ANCIENT T

RADUAN NASSAR

Ancient Tillage

*Translated from the Portuguese
by K.C.S. Sotelino*

A New Directions Paperbook Original

Originally published as *Lavoura arcaica* in 1975

Manufactured in the United States of America
New Directions Books are printed on acid-free paper
First published in 2017 as New Directions Paperbook 1366

Library of Congress Cataloging-in-Publication Data
Names: Nassar, Raduan, 1935– author. | Sotelino, Karen Sherwood, translator.
Title: Ancient tillage / by Raduan Nassar ; translated by Karen Sherwood
Sotelino.
Other titles: Lavoura arcaica. English
Description: New York : New Directions Publishing, 2017.
Identifiers: LCCN 2016041673 | ISBN 9780811226561 (acid-free paper)
Classification: LCC PQ9698.24.A838 L313 2017 | DDC 869.3/42—dc23
LC record available at https://lccn.loc.gov/2016041673

10 9 8 7 6 5 4 3 2 1

New Directions Books are published for James Laughlin
by New Directions Publishing Corporation
80 Eighth Avenue, New York 10011

ANCIENT TILLAGE

The Departure

Can we be blamed for this plant called childhood, its seduction, its vigor and earnestness? (Jorge de Lima)

1

MY EYES ON the ceiling, nudity in the room; pink, blue or violet, the impenetrable room; the individual room, a world, a cathedral room, where, during the breaks from my anguish, I gathered a rough stem into the palm of my hand, the white rose of desperation, since, among the objects the room had sanctified, the objects of the body came first; I was lying on the hardwood floor of my bedroom in an old village boarding house when my brother came to take me home; my dynamic and disciplined hand, just prior to his entrance, had been running slowly over my wet skin, my poison-filled fingertips touching the newborn fuzz on my still-warm chest; my head rolled numbly as my hair moved in thick waves over the damp curve of my forehead; I rested one of my cheeks on the floor, but my eyes grasped very little, remained practically immobile behind the swift flight of my lashes; the knocking on the door came through gently, settled in meaninglessly, like cotton-silk tufts nestling in the sinuous curves of my ear, where, for a few minutes, it slept; the repetitive noise, still soft and gentle, did not disturb my sweet drunkenness, nor my drowsiness, nor the dispersed, sparse, comfortless whirling; later my eyes saw the turning doorknob, but the spinning was forgotten inside my retina — a lifeless object, a vibrationless sound or a dark breeze in the basement of my memory; the pounding at that moment set the lethargic objects in that bedroom off balance and into desperation. I stood up lightly and silently, and bent over to pick up the towel spread out on the floor; I dried off my hands, squeezed my eyes shut, shaking my head to jar them, picked up the shirt piled on the chair, tucked my obscure, purple organ back into my slacks, and walked quickly over to open the door, using it to shield myself from view: my older brother was outside; as soon as he came in, we faced each other, our eyes absolutely still, we were separated by a space of dry earth, there was fear and wonder in that dust, but no discovery, I don't even know what there was, and we said nothing, until he held out his arms, grasping my shoulders in silence with his strong hands, and we looked at each other and in one precise second our memories stumbled and assaulted our eyes; I saw his eyes suddenly moisten, and that was when he hugged me, and I felt the weight of the entire family's soaking wet arms in his embrace; we looked at each other again, and I said, "I wasn't expecting you," was what I said, confused with the awkwardness of my words, filled with regret at letting anything at all slip out, but even so, I repeated myself, "I wasn't expecting you," was what I said once again and I felt the powerful strength of my family overrunning me like a heavy rush of water as he was saying to me, "We love you so much, we love you so much," and that was all he said as he embraced me again; still confused, dazed, I showed him to the chair in the corner, but he remained motionless and, taking his handkerchief from his pocket, he said, "Button up your shirt, André."

2

IN THE SLUGGISH, lazy afternoons on the *fazenda*, somewhere off in the woods, I would escape my family's apprehensive eyes; I would soothe my feverish feet in the moist dirt, cover my body with leaves, and, lying in the shade, I would sleep with the stillness of an ailing plant curved under the weight of a red blossom; weren't those stems surrounding me fairies, filled with patience, silently keeping vigil over my adolescent slumber? Which ancient urns were releasing the protective voices calling out to me from the veranda? What was the use of those calls, if faster, more active messengers rode the wind skillfully, cutting through the threads of the atmosphere? (When ripe, my slumber was gathered with the religious voluptuousness of gathered fruit.)

3

I RECALLED HEARING my father preach over and over again that our eyes are the lanterns of our bodies, and if they were good it was because our bodies contained light, and if our eyes were not clear it was because they revealed a dark, gloomy body, and standing there before my brother, inhaling the exalted aroma of wine, I knew my eyes were two repulsive pits, but it didn't matter to me, I was confused, even lost, and I saw myself suddenly doing things, fooling with my hands, moving about the room, as if my embarrassment grew from the disorder around me: I arranged the things on the table, spread a cloth over it, emptied the ashtray into the rubbish bin, straightened the sheets, folded the towel over the headboard, and had already returned to the table to fill two glasses when I slipped and almost asked about Ana, but it was only a sudden, stumbling impulse; what I could have asked, should have asked, was how he had found the inn, how he had discovered me in that old terraced house, or I could have tried to ingenuously discover the reason for his visit, but I wasn't even thinking about any of that; I was just dark inside, incapable of working my way out of the flesh of my feelings, and standing there at the table, the only thing I knew for certain was that my exasperated eyes were looking down on the rose-colored wine I was pouring into the glasses. "The shutters," he said, "Why are the shutters closed?" he asked from the chair in the corner where he was sitting, and I did not think twice and rushed to open the window and outside there was a tender, almost cool afternoon, made of fibrous orange sunshine, abundantly coloring my bedroom, that gloomy pond, and I was still latching the shutters when a first attack just barely ran through me — it was merely passing so I didn't pay any attention, I thought only of finishing what I was doing — and as soon as it passed, I generously, almost scornfully, went ahead and placed the sublime glass of wine in his hands; and as an impertinent breeze was billowing out the heavy lace curtains (which were adorned with two woven angels scaling clouds, their puffy cheeks blowing into serene horns), I sat heavily down on the edge of the bed, my eyes staring at the floor, two dark, shriveled holes, and I have no doubt that his light-filled eyes above me were poisoning me, and I was almost overcome by a silent, short wave that nearly made me yell "Don't worry, brother, all you have to do is hurry to find the solemn voice you're seeking, that voice strengthened by disapproval, rush into questions about what has been going on all along, try out your gestures, disagree with me to my face, shatter the family china before my eyes," just to make him angry, but I refrained, believing that to exhort him would not only be useless, but also foolish; instead, I fell to thinking about his eyes, about my mother's, in the most silent moments of the afternoon, behind which the tenderness and apprehension of an entire family were hidden, and I thought of her opening my bedroom door at odd times and the emerging of her maternal, solicitous shape, "Darling, don't stay in bed like that, don't make me suffer, speak to me," and, surprised and frightened, I felt that any minute my tears would explode, while at the same time, I thought it might be good to take advantage of the last dregs of my drunkenness that had not yet been cowed by his arrival, by confessing piously perhaps, "It's my delirium, Pedro, it's my delirium, if you want to know the truth," but this was no more than a slightly tumultuous thought flashing through my mind, making me finish off my wine in two rapid gulps, I thought it senseless to say anything at all and began hearing my brother's appropriately calm, serene voice (he was fulfilling the sublime mission of returning the wayward son to the bosom of the family) as he started speaking in prayer mode (it was my father's tone) of the stones and mortar of our cathedral.

4

SUDANESA (OR SCHUDA) was generously formed; beneath a sloping, thatched roof of thick, golden, coarse grass, she lived inside a pen built with stakes stuck firmly into the ground, one next to the other, between which I only just dared to glimpse; she gulped and swished water from a clay bowl, freshly filled every morning; she lay down and rested her head on a bed well stacked with sweet-smelling, soft hay, even as the sun outside reached high noon; her trough was always clean, filled with corn kernels and carefully picked green grass into which I rubbed parsley to stimulate her appetite; the first time I saw Sudanesa with my sickly eyes was when I brought her out one evening among the flowering bushes surrounding her courtesan's rural boudoir: I led her carefully, like a devoted lover, and she followed docilely on her high hooves, playfully, swinging her proud, ample body swaying on the pillars of her finely shaped legs; it was the body I had begun to take care of in the late afternoons, my humus-coated hands plunging into receptacles of soothing ointments with their various aromas, delving right afterward into her soft, fringed coat; but she was not a lascivious nanny goat, she was a boy's nanny goat, her contours were defined by full, bloated nipples, and with her tremors, her darkest, most private parts were exposed and she was completely susceptible to the comb running through her luxurious, bulging coat; she was a smug nanny goat, an earring-clad she-goat with a small tail, no more than a healthy, bristle-covered, wire spring, which reacted to the lightest of touches, highly sensitive to the most subtle, gentle caresses of a finger; her entire body sculpted itself while maneuvering a green stem around in her patient mouth—chewing not with her teeth, but with time; in these moments, she was made of stone, two traces of sorrow engraved in her eyes; in this mystical posture, with her long, black lashes, she was a predestined goat; Sudanesa had been brought to the *fazenda* to add new blood, though she had arrived expecting, and required special care, that was when I, a timid adolescent, took the first steps outside my solitude: I left my idleness behind and—sacrilege—appointed myself her lyric shepherd; I perfected her shape, made her coat shine and gave her flowered jewels, winding around her neck yards of creeper vine, with its brightly colored fruit dangling like bells; Schuda was patient, even more, generous, as a swollen, mysterious and lubricious stem sought, through intercourse, the concurrence of her body.

5

LOVE, UNION, AND our work alongside our father was
the message of austere purity stored safely in our shrines,
solemnly absorbed at daily communion, in the making of
our morning breakfast and within our evening scripture;
without losing sight of the pious clarity of this maxim, my
brother proceeded with his sermon, discreetly reminding
me, each step of the way, of my immaturity in life, speaking
of the mishaps to which everyone is vulnerable, and saying
that it was normal that this should have happened, but it
was also important to bear in mind the unique emotional
and spiritual ties that bound us, which would prevent us
from ever succumbing to temptation and which guarded us
against a fall (no matter what its nature); at the very least,
each family member had to do his part to be responsible for
and look after these ties, each family member had to uphold
his share, since if only one member were to make a false
move, the entire family would topple; he said that as long

as the house stood, each one of us also stood, and to keep the house from falling, our sense of obligation must be strengthened constantly, we must worship our blood ties, never wander beyond our doorway, always answer our father when he spoke, never avert our eyes from a brother in need, participate in the work of the family, bring fruit into the home and help to replenish the common table; thus, within the austerity of our way of life there would always be room for a great deal of happiness, beginning with the fulfilment of our individually assigned tasks, since a person would be condemned to bear a terrible burden were he to shirk the sacred demands of his duties; he went on to say that everyone at home had their own desires, but nevertheless, evil impulses must be restrained, all the while those that were good should be moderated prudently, without ever losing sight of the balance, cultivating self-control, protecting oneself from egoism and the dangerous passion by which it is accompanied, seeking solutions to personal problems without creating more serious problems for loved ones, and he reminded me that to think through any given situation the same solid trunk, faithful hand, loving word and wise principles had always been there, and that life's horizon was not as expansive as some tend to believe; in my case, the happiness I had imagined existed beyond our father's realm was no more than an illusion; disavowing the irreverent reasons for my flight (although suggesting discreetly my steps had set a bad example for Lula, the youngest in the family, whose eyes were glued to my every move), my brother blew hot wind into his sermon by telling me there was more strength in the pardon than in the offence itself, and more strength in the mending than in the misguided ways, leaving it very clear that these should be the two sublime counterparts to any fine character, the former represented by my family upon my return, and the latter— the mending of ways—represented by me, the wayward son: "You've no idea what we've been going through in your absence, you'd be shocked at the worn faces of our family; it's difficult for me to tell you this, brother, but Mother can no longer hide her sobbing," he said, blending a sort of increasingly tense feeling of tenderness with his reprimand; he was moving along serenely and surely, somewhat solemnly (like my father), all the while, I was succumbing to rapid vertigo, conjuring up the meager provisions of this poor family of ours, now deprived of its former strength, and in my darkness, I may just have had a flash of lucidity, as I suspected that, in their lack of spiritual sustenance, the last few seeds from the family fields were being cooked, over a will-o'-the-wisp glow, in a prosaic boarding-house room: "She told no one you had left, at lunch that day each of us at the table felt, more than the next, the weight of your empty chair; but we remained silent, staring at our plates as Mother served us, not one of us had the courage to ask where you were, our afternoon of work with Father dragged on, our thoughts were with our sisters at home busily working in the kitchen or embroidering on the veranda, stitching at the sewing machine, or cleaning out the pantry; no matter where the girls were, they were transformed that very day; no longer filling the house with joy, having already given in to their sense of abandonment and discomfort; you should have been there, André, you should have; and you should have seen our father locked up in his silence: as soon as dinner was over, he left the table and went to the veranda; no one saw him withdraw, he stood there next to the railing, watching who knows what in the darkness; only at bedtime, when I went into your room and opened your closet and empty drawers did I understand, as the eldest brother, the scope of what had happened: the beginning of the disintegration of the family," he said, then stopped, and I knew why, I had only to look at his face, but I did not, for there were also things inside me to be seen, and I could have said "The disintegration of the family started long before you think, in my childhood, when faith grew virulently inside me and when I had so much more passion than anyone else in the house," is what I could have said, with certainty, but it was no time to speculate on the obscure methods of faith, to take up its dissolute aspects, the sacramental consumption of blood and flesh, to investigate the voluptuousness and tremors of devotion, but even so I started to remember my Marian society ribbon, to recall that, as a pious child, I would set it next to my bed before sleeping and also, how God would wake me up daily at five o'clock for early communion, and I would lie awake, sadly watching my brothers in their beds as they slept through my bliss, I would amuse myself as shadows broke through the dawn, and with each ray of daylight shining through the cracks, I would rediscover the magical fantasy of the small figures painted up high on the wall like a border, just waiting for her to come into the bedroom and whisper again and again, "Wake up, sweetheart," gently touching me again and again, until I, pretending all the while that I was sleeping, would grasp her hands with a shiver and they in turn would play their subtly composed game beneath the covers, and I would laugh and she would lovingly remind me in a whisper not to "wake up your brothers, sweetheart," and she would hold my head against the warm pillow of her stomach, and bending her full body, she would kiss my hair again and again, and as soon as I got up, God was right next to me on my bedside table and it was a god I could grasp in my hands and put around my neck, filling my chest, and as a young boy I would enter the church like a balloon, the domestic light of our childhood was good, the homemade bread on our table, the hot milk and coffee and the butter dish; that luminous clarity of our home always seemed brighter when we would return from the village, the clarity that was later to perturb me so, making me strange and mute, leaving me prostrate in bed, like a convalescent, from the time of my adolescence onward; "Things we never suspected within the limits of our home" almost slipped out, but once again I believed it would have been useless to say anything, in fact I felt incapable of saying anything at all, and, lifting my eyes, I saw that my brother's gaze was immersed in his glass, and motionless; as if in response to the message in my expression, he said, "The more rigid the structure, the harder the fall, the strength and the joy of a family can disappear thus in one fell swoop," is what he said, as a sudden look of mourning crossed his face, and then he interrupted himself, and instantaneously my imagination was flooded with the bright Sunday gatherings when our city relatives and friends would visit us, and in the woods behind the house, beneath the tallest trees, which along with the sun made up a gentle, joyous play of shadow and light, after the smell of the roasted meat had been long lost among the many leaves on the fullest branches, and the tablecloth, previously laid over the calm lawn, folded away, I would curl up near a distant tree trunk, from where I could follow the tumultuous group of boys and girls busily getting things ready for the dance, among whom were my sisters with their country ways, wearing their light, bright dresses, full of love's promise suspended within the purity of a greater love, running gracefully, covering the woods with their laughter, carrying the baskets of fruit over to the same place where the cloth had been, the melons and watermelons split open, with gales of laughter, and the grapes and oranges picked from the orchards lushly displayed in these baskets, a centerpiece suggesting the theme of the dance, and this joy was sublime, along with the setting sun, porous beams of divine light easing their way between the leaves and branches, occasionally spilling over into the peaceful shadows and reverberating intensely on those damp faces, and the men's circle would then start to form, my father, his sleeves rolled up, would gather the youngest, who would join arms stiffly, their fingers firmly intertwined, making up the solid contour of a circle around the fruit, as if it were the strong, clear contour of an oxcart wheel, and soon my elderly uncle, the old immigrant, a pastor in his youth, would take his flute from his pocket, a delicate stem in his heavy hands, and would begin to blow into it like a bird, his cheeks inflating like those of a child, and his cheeks would swell so much, would get so puffy and flushed, it seemed as if all his wine would flow from his ears, as if from a faucet, and with the sound of the flute, the circle would begin to move slowly, almost obstinately, first in one direction, and then in the other, gradually trying out its strength in a stiff coming and going to the rhythm of the strong, muffled sound of the virile stomping, until suddenly the flute would fly, cutting enchantingly into the woods, traversing the blossoming grasses and sweeping the pastures, and the now vibrant wheel would speed up, its movement circumscribing the entire circle, which was no longer an oxcart wheel, but a huge mill wheel, spinning swiftly in one direction, and at the trill of the flute, in the other, and the elderly, who stood by watching, and the young girls, who awaited their turn, would all clap, strengthening the new rhythm, and before long, Ana would impatiently and impetuously sweep into the dancing circle with her country-girl figure and a red flower, like a drop of blood, holding her loose dark hair to one side; this sister of mine who, more than anyone else in the house, was diseased in body, as was I, and right away I could sense her precise, gypsy steps moving about the circle, dexterously and curvaceously weaving her way through the baskets of fruit and flowers, touching the earth only with the tips of her bare feet, her arms lifted above her head in languishing, serpentine movements to the slowest, most undulating melody of the flute, her graceful hands twisting and turning up in the air; she would be overtaken with wild elegance, her melodious fingers snapping, as if they were, as if they had been the first ever castanets, and the circle surrounding her would pick up speed deliriously, the clapping hands outside would grow increasingly hot and strong, then suddenly and impetuously, magnetizing everyone, she would grab a white handkerchief from one of the boys' pockets, waving it with her hand above her head while she kept up her serpentine movements; this sister of mine knew what she was about, first hiding her venom well concealed beneath her tongue, then biting into the grapes, which hung in saliva-drenched bunches, she would dance amongst them all, rendering life more turbulent, stirring up pain, drawing out cries of exaltation; and presently, harmonizing in a strange language, the elders would begin to sing out simple verses, almost like chants, and a young mischievous cousin, caught up in the current, would make strident cymbals out of two pan lids and it would seem as if, following the contagious music, the herons and teals had flown in from the lake to join everyone there in the woods, and I could imagine, his solemnity dampened by wine, my father's joyful eyes, reassured that not everything on board was to rot under the hatches; and sitting on an exposed root over in a shady corner of the woods, I would let the light wind blowing through the trees flow through my shirt, inflating my chest, and feel the soft caress of my own hair on my forehead, and from a distance, in this apparently relaxed position, I would imagine the lavender aroma of her fresh complexion, the full tenderness of her mouth, like a piece of sweet orange, and the mystery and malice in her date-like eyes; my staring was unabashed, I would untie my shoes, take off my socks and, with my clean, white feet, scrape away the dry leaves to the layer of thick humus below, and my unrestrained desire was to dig into the earth with my

nails and to lie down in this pit and cover myself with the
damp earth, and lost on this secluded trail I wouldn't per-
ceive when she would leave the others, searching everywhere with her wide, worried eyes, and the sound of her
footsteps, as she came closer, would mingle with the onset
of the sudden, timid noise of the small animals stirring al-
luringly and affectionately nearby, so I would only notice
her presence as she approached, and then I would look
down and concentrate on her steps, which were suddenly
no longer rushed, but slow and heavy, distinctly smashing
the dry leaves beneath her feet and smashing me confusedly
within, and bowing my head, I would soon feel her warm,
caring hand first removing a particle of dirt, then gathering
and smoothing out my hair, and her voice, born of her calci-
fied womb, would suddenly gush into the depth of my sanc-
tuary, and it was as if it came from a temple built only of
stones, yet filled with porous light beaming through stained
glass, "Come, sweetheart, come and play with your brothers
and sisters," and quietly curled up in my spot I would merely
say "Leave me alone, Mother, I'm having fun," but my bitter
eyes would never leave my sister, the soles of her feet aflame,
branding and burning inside me … what bright dust, as I
see the last of that distant time, the same period when, one
day, with chained feet, I averted my eyes to avoid her face;
my pack, fixed firmly to my back, weighing heavily on me
as I left the house, the two of us walking like twins sharing

shoulders, twin yolks from the same egg, one with eyes facing forward, the other, backward; standing there looking at my brother, I was seeing so many faraway things, and that evening I embarked on my desperate decision to throw myself into the soft stomach of the moment; who knows, I still might have even asked my brother, in a kindly impulse, to leave and to "Give my best to the family," closing the door behind him; then, alone in my darkness, I would roll myself up in the soft layer of sunlight hanging on one of the bedroom walls, and protected inside that blanket, I would eventually surrender to wine and to my fortune.

6

FROM THE TIME I left home, it was by stifling my revolt
(my silence was bruising! my anger was textured!) that
step by step I distanced myself from the *fazenda*; and if
perchance I were to become distracted and ask "Where are
we going?'—it made no difference that in looking around I
perceived very new, perhaps less harsh landscapes, it made
no difference that my walking led me to increasingly remote
regions, because I could hear the rigid judgment clearly,
even as it emerged from my longing, like gravel, or a brittle
bone, devoid of any doubt whatsoever—"We're forever on
our way home."

7

"WHEN I SAID I was going to bring you home, she held still and her eyes brimmed with water, fear was in those eyes, 'Come on, Mother,' I said, 'Try to cheer up, you should laugh, Mum,' I said, tussling her hair, 'don't act like that, and don't worry, I promise there will be no arguing with that renegade, you'll see how happy he'll be, you'll see,' I told her, 'Mother, you'll see how everything is going to be like it was, just like it used to be,' I said and she held me, and as she held me she merely said, 'Bring him back, Pedro, bring him back, and don't tell your brother, nor your sisters that you're going, but bring him back,' and while I was saying, 'Stop it, Mum, stop it,' she went on to say, 'Now I'm going to go knead sweet rolls, the kind he used to like so much,' she said, holding me as if she were holding you, André," and my brother smiled, his washed-out eyes filled with light, with the most tender, cloudless expression in the world, but this didn't really move me, I remained quiet, and in my moist memory I could only recall her pulling me out of bed and dragging me into the kitchen, "Come on, sweetheart, come with me," and, standing near the table holding my hand in one of hers while she reached with the fingertips of the other deeply into the bowl, she would get a mouthful of food to feed me, not with a fork, but with those thick fingers, "Like you feed a lamb," she would always say, and hearing my brother say, suddenly reserved, "She's aged tremendously," I continued to think of her in the other direction and I could see her sitting in her rocking chair, absolutely alone and lost in her gray daydreams, from the earliest hours of the day unraveling the lace of love and family unity woven over a lifetime, and seeing the comb in her hair buried into the bun at the nape of her neck, in majestic simplicity, it seemed right then that it was worth an entire history book, and I also felt, thinking about her, that the fruit growing in my throat was about to burst, and it was not just any fruit, but a fig dripping thick honey, filling my lungs, already rising sumptuously to my eyes, but with great effort, by lowering my eyelids, I closed all my pores, although it was totally pointless, since nothing kept my brother from his indefatigable tillage: "But no one at home has changed as much as Ana," he said, "as soon as you left she shut herself up in prayer in the chapel; when she is not wandering aimlessly in the most remote parts of the woods, she's sort of hidden, somewhat strangely, over by the old house; no one at home is able to bring her out of her pious silence; she always wears a veil over her head and she spends all day wandering around the *fazenda* barefoot, like a sleepwalker; no one at home causes us more worry," he said, and suddenly I saw my room darken, and I knew only that darkness, the darkness against which I always closed my eyes in fear, which is why I stood up, reacting to the dizziness I was beginning to feel, and on the pretext of refilling our glasses, I stepped haltingly over to the table to get another bottle, but as soon as I made a move to pour more wine, I saw the gesture of his hand, like my father's; "I won't have any more," he said gravely, resolutely, strangely changed, "nor should you drink any more, it is not from this wine that the wisdom of our father's lessons comes forth," he said, frowning, with a sudden trace of anger, having decidedly resigned from breaking my silence with affection, and making it clear that from that point on I was to be submitted to a harsh reprimand: "It is not the spirit of this wine that will repair so much damage in our home—" he continued cuttingly— "put the bottle away, refrain from debauchery, we're talking about the family," he went on, cruelly, openly hostile, suddenly making me feel that the dog forever stretched out in the sleepy shadow of the eaves was getting away from me, escaping its leash and making me feel that any restraint and sobriety at that moment deserved my most sarcastic scorn and, in a flash of light, making me feel what a generous, abundant gift it would be to simply plunge from the ceiling, I felt all of that and much more with the trembling that overtook my entire body in a tormented spasm, "It's all right for us to have a drink," I yelled, transformed, the transformation that should have happened at home years before, "I'm an epileptic," I exploded, in my worst convulsion ever, and with that violent rush flooding my veins, "an epileptic," I yelled and sobbed to myself, well aware that, at extreme risk, and cutting away at my palms, I was throwing the jug of my former identity to the ground, the jug worked from the clay of my own hands, and hurling myself flat on my face onto that shard-ridden floor, I kept shouting insanely, "Your brother is an epileptic, let it be known, go home now and make this revelation, go now and you will see the doors and windows of the house banging shut with the wind of this knowledge, and you, the men of the family, wearing hoods and carrying our father's heavy toolbox, will surround the house outside, violently hammering and nailing planks into crosses against the shutters, and our sisters dressed in black, true to their Mediterranean background, will rush around the house in a flurry of mourning, and the dance of this imprisoned family will be accompanied by a chorus of howling, whimpering and sighing, and finally, our sisters, sobbing wearily, in a flight of handkerchiefs to hide their faces, will go off and huddle in the corner and you will scream at them ever more loudly, 'Our brother is a convulsive, possessed epileptic!' and go ahead and tell them that I chose a boardinghouse room for my fits and also say, 'We lived with him and never knew, never ever suspected,' then you can all call out at once, 'He tricked us! He tricked us!' and yell as much as you want, gorge yourselves on this renewed knowledge, even if you aren't aware of the sinister web in which I was caught, and you, as the eldest brother, can howl in a desperate moan, 'It's so sad that he has our blood,' then cry out, 'He's been possessed by cursed pestilence,' and scream, 'Such disgrace has befallen our household,' and ask furiously, as if saying the rosary, 'What makes him different?' and you'll hear the somber, hoarse chorus from the shapeless mass huddled in the corner, 'He's possessed by the devil,' and go ahead and say, 'His eyes are somber,' and you'll keep hearing, 'He's possessed by the devil,' and you'll continue mouthing those gutter beads and then say in amazement and fear, 'What a heinous crime he's committed! He's possessed by the devil,' and then say, 'He's tainted the family, condemned us to burn up in flaming shame,' and you'll keep hearing the same cavernous, hollow sound, 'He's possessed by the devil! He's possessed by the devil!' and in a clamor, as if in blasphemy, raise your arms and cry out to heaven in unison, 'He has abandoned us, he has abandoned us,' and afterward, after so much lamentation, so much sobbing and grinding of teeth, and after flaunting the hair on your chest and your arms, right afterward, go directly to the linen closet, and check quickly behind the doors, take up the finely woven old sheets, and even these, like everything else in our house, even those carefully washed, folded, white cloths, everything, Pedro, everything in our house is morbidly soaked with Father's words; Father always said, he always said, Pedro, 'We must begin with the truth and finish the same way,' he was always saying things like that, those family sermons were heavy, but he always laid the foundations in the same way, with the same blocks of words, those were the rocks we tripped over as children, the stones that forever grazed us, that's where our thrashings and these marks on our bodies came from, look, Pedro, look at my arms; but he also said, probably unaware of what he was saying and certainly not realizing how one of us would use it one day, he also said carelessly, in an aside, 'Look at the strength of the tree growing in isolation and the shade it provides for the herd, and the troughs, the long troughs emerging in isolation from the immense fields, so smooth from so many tongues, where the cattle come to feed on the salt provided to purify their meat and hides,' he was always saying things like that, in his unique syntax, hard and stiffened by the sun and rain, he was the toughened farmer tilling the earth, ploughing up the shapeless rock he did not realize was so malleable in each of our hands; Pedro, the hallways of our house were confused, but that was how he wanted it, to injure the family's hands with coarse rocks, to scrape our blood as you would limestone, but did it ever occur to you, did it ever cross your mind, for even a second, to lift the lid of the bath-room hamper? Did you ever think of delving in with pre-carious hands and carefully removing each and every article thrown inside? I would drag up a piece of each one of us when I dug in there, no one heard all of our cries better than I did, I can assure you, the exasperation of the family was laid to rest in the guarded silence of the intimate articles thrown in there, but you had only to look, to lift the lid and stick your hands in, it was enough to plunge your hands inside to realize how ambivalently they were used, the men's handkerchiefs, which had been extended like trays to pro-tect the purity of the sheets, all you had to do was put your hands in to gather up the wrinkled sleep of the nightgowns and pajamas and to discover, lost in their folds, the coiled, repressed energy of the most tender pubic hair, you didn't even need to rummage very much to find the periodic, walnut-colored stains on the women's intimate cloth pads, nor to hear the mute, scrotum-flowing cries that starched the men's soft white cotton underwear, you had to know the body of the entire family, to hold the red-dust-covered sanitary napkins in your hands, as if they were an assassin's rags, to know the family's every mood moldering away in the vinegary, rotten smell of the cold, vein-ridden walls of a dirty clothes hamper; no one stuck their hands inside there more than I did, Pedro, no one felt the stains of loneliness more than I did, many of them aborted, greased by the imagination, you had to catch the charnel house off-guard, when it was snoring, leave your bed and venture through the hallways, listen to the throbbing behind all the doors, the trembling, the moaning and the soft voluptuousness of our homicidal plans, no one heard each of us at home better than I did, Pedro, no one loved each of us more, nor better knew the pathway to our union, the pathway along which we were led steadily by the image of our grandfather, the tall, slender old man carved from the wood of the family furniture; he was the one, Pedro, the truth is, he was the one running through our ancestral veins, always in the same black suit, bulky on his thin, skeletal body, depravedly baring the dry, white skin of his face; the truth is, he led us, forever locked up inside his own vest, his pocket-watch chain tracing an enormous, shiny golden hook on his dark chest, the old ascetic, the farmer worked from ancestral hay, who on drowsy afternoons of days gone by would store his dehydrated sleep inside the hampers and carefully lined drawers of our bureaus, and who would allow himself no more than the gentle, lyrical mystery of a memory-filled, dream-laden jasmine tucked into his lapel on hot, humid evenings, he was the one who directed the steps we took in unison, it was always Grandfather, Pedro, he was forever inside the silence of the china cupboards, the lost promise of the hallways, making us hide our childhood fears behind

doors, never allowing us, except in contained gulps, to absorb the funereal perfume of our pain which emanated
from his solemn wanderings through the old house; he was
a plaster-carved guide, that eyeless grandfather of ours, Pedro, nothing more than two deep, hollow, somber cavities
in his face, nothing more, Pedro, nothing else shone on that
bony stalk besides the chain of his terrible, golden, oriental
hook," I said, screaming and shaking, and reading the surprise, fear, terror and absolute whiteness all over his face, I
still managed to cry out, "Plug your ears, stick your fingers
in the holes," and, having run from one corner of the room
to the other in possessed frenzy, I suddenly dropped to my
knees, sat back on my heels and, seeing his trembling hand,
he himself now filling our glasses, I was overcome with
doubt whether to bash him in the face or kiss his cheeks;
and for a moment, we fell into a taut silence in order that
nothing disturb the current of my trance; between massive
gulps of wine, contemplating both the ceiling of my room
and the dark things I could see inside my brother's mouth,
I noticed how carefully he was trying to compose a look and
a stance conducive to my carrying on; I wanted to say,
"Don't worry, brother, don't worry, because I am able to
resume my fit," after all, what was the point of talking further? For me, the world had already been laid bare, I had
only to take in a deep breath, take up the wine from the

depth of the bottle, and bathe all my words in that sweet
indolence, feel each drop all the way to the back of my
tongue, each crushed grape from that wine, from that divine spirit; "It is my delirium, Pedro," I said in a warm wave,
"It's my delirium," I repeated, and it occurred to me that
perhaps I was already in communion with the oily saliva of
that word, but in fact, I was only feeling the first reverbera-
tions of my own red blood, salty and thick as it circulated in
my head, inflating the formerly feeble flower, transforming
that pile of worms into a sacred pillow, stripped of trim-
mings, on which I could rest my thoughts; at that foamy
moment, only I knew the waters, the waves on which I was
sailing, only I knew the salty vertigo causing my oscillation,
"It's my delirium," I said, on a still darker wave, tired of
soothing thoughts, affectionate eyes and gentle contor-
tions; would that everything burn, my feet, the thorns in my
arms, the leaves that covered my wooden body, my forehead and lips, so long as at the same time my useless tongue
be spared; the rest, later, it mattered very little that later the
rest be lost among the family's tears, sobbing and trembling; "Pedro, my brother, our father's sermons were incon-
sistent," I said suddenly with a rebel's frivolity, sensing, if
only for a fleeting moment, his hand in awkward prepara-
tion for a reproachful gesture: instead it was withdrawn,
anxiously and silently, the frightened hands of the family
leaving the sermon-fed table; the faces surrounding that

table of our adolescence were so curdled: Father, at the head of it, the wall clock behind him, each and every one of his words weighed by the pendulum, with nothing distracting us more at that time than the deep bells marking the passing of the hours.

8

WHERE WAS MY head? What kind of hay made up this bed, the softest, most sweet-smelling, restful hay where I laid my head, way at the back of the stables and corrals? Which hay was this that protected me while I rested, numbed by the thick tongue of a doting cow gnawing caressingly at my tingling skin? What sort of hay was this, carrying me off to calm dreams, buoying me up over my burning nettles, lulled by the breeze in this immense blanket of flowering pasture? What kind of light, youthful sleep was this, suckling upon only the most delicious orchard juices? What kind of luscious fruits were these, so softly resistant as my drowsy teeth bit and pulled at them? What were these white, angelic kernels shelling out placid smiles, if horseflies escaped my lips in my greenish dreams? Such a hidden, patient seed! Such a long hibernation! Such a forgotten sun, such an adolescent bullock, such abandoned slumber amidst fenceposts and lowing! Where was my head? That is my only question throughout the sleepless early morning hours when I open my window and feel like setting thick candles in rows and lighting them on the wings of the damp, silent blue breeze that soars like a scarf over the atmosphere at the same time every day; wasn't my slumber, like old fruit, made up entirely of ripened hours? Which resins were dissolved in that furious air, slyly thrashing the delicate grasses of my nostrils? Which startling, hot breath suddenly opened my eyelashes? Which abrupt, restless colt was carrying my body off in galloping levitation? These are the questions I keep asking one after another, without knowing to whom I am speaking, carving up the earth in the early morning light from my window, like a laborer gone mad who, in the coldest hours of dawn, removes the blankets of the womb and, barefoot and on an empty stomach, starts lining up stone blocks on a shelf; the bed was not made of hay, it was a bed well hardened by compost, with a pillow made of manure, where a most improbable plant grows, a certain mushroom, where a certain poisonous flower blooms virulently, breaking through the moss of the elders' texts; this primeval dust, the nuclear bud, engendered in underground furrows and bursting from soft, imaginative earth. "Such suffering, such suffering, such terrible suffering!" I confessed, gleaning from these words the useless liqueur I was distilling, yet what sweet bitterness it was to speak out, tracing the symmetry of a flower patch on to a bed of silence, the winding stone pathways of a garden lawn, driving eucalyptus stakes around seedbeds, digging the entrance to a brickyard with bare hands, building up a damp dung wall, and in this harmoniously fathomed silence, which smelled of wine, and of manure, to compose time, patiently.

9

THE FACES SURROUNDING the table of our adolescence were so curdled: Father at the head, the wall clock behind him, each and every one of his words weighed by the pendulum, with nothing distracting us more at that time than the deep bells marking the passing hours: "Time is the greatest treasure available to man; although not consumable, time is our most valuable nourishment; even if immeasurable, time is still our largest gift; it has neither beginning nor end; it is an exotic apple that cannot be split in pieces, although it provides for the entire world equally; omnipresent, time is everywhere; time exists, for example, in this old table: first there was the generous earth, then the centennial tree born from the passing of calm years, and finally, the knotty, hard plank, worked day after day by the artisan's hand; time is in the chairs on which we sit, in all our other furniture, in the walls of our house, in the water we drink, the plentiful earth, the sprouting seed, the fruit we harvest, the bread on our table, in the fertile dough of our bodies, in the light by which we are illuminated, in everything that goes through our minds, in the scattered dust, as in everything else that surrounds us; the man who collects money and measures his own worth by its weight is not rich, nor is the man who spreads himself out dissolutely over vast tracts of land; the only rich man is the man who has learned to live piously and humbly with time, approaching it gently, never contradicting its moods, never getting off course, nor disrupting its current, always aware of its tide, always welcoming it wisely to receive its favors, not its wrath; life is essentially held in balance by this supreme gift, and when seeking, those who find the right pace, know when to wait, and how much time to give things, never risk tripping up in error; that is why no one in our household ever oversteps himself: to overstep is to omit the time needed for our pursuit; and no one in our household ever puts the cart before the horse: to put the cart before the horse would be to withhold the amount of time the task requires; and furthermore, no one in our household would ever start building from the roof down: to start to build from the roof down would be to eliminate the time it would take to lay the foundations and construct the walls of a house; if you exceed the limits of time and rush anxiously and boldly ahead of yourself, you will never get your due, for only the true measure of time reveals the true nature of things; if you gulp down the entire glass, you will never taste the wine; and if you find the right balance, you will be spared ruin and disappointment, it is in the magical wielding of this scale wherein lies the mathematics of the wise, in one dish, a coarse, malleable mass, in the other, enough time to allow each and every one the perfect calculation, watch carefully, intervene quickly at the slightest imbalance; the crude hands of the fishmonger weighing his pungent catch are wise: firm and controlled, through concise calculation, they glean absolute repose from the two hanging dishes, the perfection of immobility; this rare result is achieved only by those who allow no malignant tremor to take over their hands, nor to rise and corrupt the blessed strength of their arms, nor to spread and reach throughout the pure regions of their bodies, nor to cause their heads to swell with pestilence, clouding their eyes with turmoil and darkness; we cannot get into our stirrups while they are still on the anvil, nor can we weave our bridles from flaming fiber, and to where, might we ask, is the rider on the wild colt rushing off? The world of passion is an unbalanced world, and it is against this world that we must stretch the wires of our fences, and on the barbs of these endless wires, tightly weave our netting wherein to entwine our dense, vigorous hedge that it may separate and protect the calm, bright light of our house, that it may cover and hide from our eyes the burning darkness on the other side; and let not one of us trespass this boundary, nor even cast our glance beyond, let none among us ever fall into this frenzied, boiling cauldron, where frivolous chemistry attempts to dissolve and recreate time; to abuse this transforming substance, destined to be used by time alone, will lead to sure punishment, and to challenge time will only result in its implacable blow; woe unto those who play with fire: their hands will fill with ashes; woe unto those who allow themselves to be sucked into the warmth of the flames: they will be cursed with insomnia; woe unto those who rest their backs on these tarnished logs: they will secrete pus daily; woe unto those who fall and let go: they will burn to the raw; woe unto those whose throats burn from so much screaming: they will be heard, for all their sobbing; woe unto those who rush through the process of change: their hands will be bloodstained; woe unto those who are lascivious, who yearn to see and feel everything intensely: their hands will be filled with plaster, or with bone dust, cold and white—who knows, maybe even deathlike—but at the very least, the absolute negation of so much color and intensity: they will end up seeing nothing from wanting to see so much; feeling nothing, from wanting to feel so much, atoning for wanting to live so much; and if you are passionate, you had better be careful, avert your eyes from the rust-red dust that they not be blurred, remove the scarabs from your ears, which cause confusion and turmoil, and purge the cursed, poisonous lime from the fluid in your glands; build a fence around your body, or simply shield it, these are the skills we must use to prevent the darkness on one side from invading and contaminating the light on the other, after all, what strength is there in the gale sweeping across the floor and prowling all over the house like a ghost if we do not expose our eyes to its dust? Through isolation we will escape the danger of passion, yet let no one understand by this that we should merely cross our arms, since the devil's weeds flourish on idle land: no one in our household should cross his arms while there is land to be tilled, no one in our household should cross his arms when there are walls to be raised, and no one in our household should cross his arms when a brother is in trouble; we must be forthright in our dealings with time, for it is as capricious as a child, yet we must be humble and docile in confronting its will, abstaining from action when time calls for contemplation, acting only when it so requires, for time knows kindness, time is vast, time is great, time is generous, time is abundant, always bountiful with its deliverance: time soothes our afflictions, eases the tension of the worried, relieves the pain of the tortured, brings light to those who live in darkness, spirit to the indifferent, comfort to the mourning, joy to the sorrowful, consolation to the forsaken, relaxation to the writhing, serenity to the uneasy, rest to the restless, peace to the stricken, moisture to withered souls; time satisfies moderate appetites, quells thirst and hunger, gives lifeblood to those in need, and moreover, entertains everyone with its playthings; it attends to our every need, but our painful desire will only find blessed relief through obedience to this implacable law: absolute servitude to the incontestable sovereignty of time, bowing down in this remarkable worship; our purification comes through patience, we must bathe ourselves in gentle waters, soaking our bodies in placated minutes, religiously enjoying the intoxication of waiting, while tirelessly partaking of this abundant, universal fruit, absorbing the juice contained in every last grape to the point of exhaustion, for we can only mature through this exercise, building our own immortality with discipline, and, if we are wise, in so doing we will forge a paradise of gentle fantasies where otherwise there would have been a wretched universe, filled with hope and all its pain; wisdom is found in the sweetness of old age and the empty chair at the opposite end of this very table is our example: our roots are found in Grandfather's memory, in the patriarch who fed on salt and water in order to provide us with the cleansed Word, in the patriarch whose mineral cleanliness of thought was never disturbed by the convulsions of nature; not one of us should ever erase the memory of his handsome, aged features, nor the memory of his gaunt discretion as he pon-

dered away the time in his wanderings about the house; nor
the memory of his delicate leather boots, the squeaking of
the floorboards in the hallways, and perhaps most important of all, the slow, measured steps that halted only when
Grandfather, reaching with two fingers into his vest pocket,
would carefully remove and calmly read his watch, placed
in his hand as if in prayer; the patience earnestly cultivated .
by our forebears must be the first law of this household, the
austere beam sustaining us in both adversity and hope, and
this is why I say there is no room for blasphemy in our
home, not on account of a joyful day which has been long
in coming, not for a precipitant day of calamity, not because
of late rains, nor for terrible droughts that set our crops
ablaze; no matter what the setback, there will be no blasphemy; if the litters do not thrive, if the cattle waste away, if
the eggs do not hatch, if the fruit shrivels, if the earth delays,
if the seeds do not sprout, if the stalks do not swell, if the
cluster drops, if the corn does not flower, if the grains decay,
if the harvest goes to weed, if the crops wither, if voracious
locust clouds darken our fields, if storms wield their wrath
on the family labors; and if some day a pestilent gust of
wind invades our carefully sealed boundaries, reaching the
surroundings of our home, seeping slyly through the slits in
our doors and windows, catching a member of our family
unawares, no hand in our household will clench into a fist
against the stricken brother: each one of us will look more

sweetly than ever upon the suffering brother, and each of us will offer the brother in need a kindly hand, each of us will inhale his virulent odor, and the gentleness of each heart will anoint his wounds, and our lips will tenderly kiss his disturbed hair, for love within the family means extreme patience; the father and mother, the parents and children, the brother and sister: the culmination of our principles is found in the union of the family; and every once in a while, each one in the family should take time from more urgent tasks to sit down on a bench with one foot planted squarely on the ground, and bending over, your elbow resting on your knee and head resting on the back of your hand, with gentle eyes, you should observe the movement of the sun, the wind and the rain, and with these same gentle eyes, observe time's mysterious manipulation of the other tools it wields to effect all transformations, and you must never once question its unfathomable, sinuous designs, just as upon observing the pure geometry of the plains, you would never question the winding trails shaped by the trampling of the herds out to pasture: for the cows always head for the trough, the cows always head for the watering pit; and we should be able to say the same about the ways of the family: we count on strongly built foundations, strongly erected walls and a strongly supported ceiling: patience is the virtue of all virtues, he who despairs is not wise, he who does not submit is foolish." Then Father, at the head of the table, would pause with his customary curtness and intensity, so that we could measure his majestic, rustic posture in silence: his wooden chest beneath the thick, clean cotton, his solid neck supporting his grave head, and his broad hands holding the edge of the table firmly as if they were holding the edge of a pulpit; then, drawing the light nearer, his face now coated in a slab of copper light, with his solid fingers, he would open the old booklet of texts gathered together and written out in his large, angular, hard handwriting, and he would begin, solemnly and steadily, "Once upon a time, there was a starving man."

10

(FUSING TOGETHER THE glass and metals in my cornea, and tossing out a handful of sand to blind the atmosphere, sometimes I embark on slumber already slept, and through this blurry filter, I discern rudimentary dust, a grindstone, a wooden mortar, an aged masher, extended clotheslines, troughs, ulcerous and worm-eaten from the endless strain of drudgery, a dented cup, in the shadows, a clay jug, perpetually chipped at the spout, and a coffee roaster, cylindrical, smoky, darkened and lamentable, still lethargically cranking away in my memory; I keep on drawing from the well: clay pots, a gourd salt cellar on the windowsill, a diligent milk churn on the doorstep, a clothes iron out in the wind, trying to recover its fever, an agate jug, a woodburning stove, an enormous, shallow bowl, a taciturn, iron tea pot brooding all day long over the stove; and, from the same bag, I could also take a goat-hide at the foot of the bed, a simple china dish adorning the parlor, a "Last Supper" hanging on the wall, the white covers on the backs of the cane chairs, a curvaceous hat rack, an old picture frame, a brownish wedding photograph taken with an imaginary background, and I still could draw on many other tiny, powerful fragments that I save in the same trench, as the zealous guardian of the family possessions.)

11

"I HADN'T LEFT home yet, Pedro, but Mother's eyes already reflected her suspicion of my departure," I said to my brother, when the initial turmoil of his presence in that boardinghouse room had subsided, "when I went to her, I wanted to tell her, 'Mother, say your good-byes now without knowing me, and it occurred to me that I could also say, all I did was nestle in your straw womb for nine months and be touched sweetly with your hands and mouth for many years, it was no more than that'; I wanted to say, this is the reason I'm leaving home, this is why I'm going away; so many things, Pedro, I could have told her so many things, but at the time, I could already see old artisans' prudent hands pointing toward stones and strange, charred landscapes that calloused and thickened the soles of my clay feet; of course, I could have said a lot of things to Mother, but I thought it useless to say anything, it makes no sense, I thought, to leave an exasperated carnation stem in those poor, flour-coated hands, it makes no sense, I thought again, to stain her apron by cutting the cord, slashing the bloody noonday sun, it makes no sense, I thought once again, to tear up sheets and petals, to burn hair and other leaves, filling my drastically carved mouth with the exposed ashes of the family, and that's why, instead of saying, 'Mother, you don't know me,' I thought it better to stay on that limestone trail, even though I was thirsty, my mouth, dry and salty, I thought it was better to remain locked up before her, like someone with nothing, and in fact I had nothing to say to her; she wanted to say something, and I thought, 'Mother has something to say that I might listen to, something to say, perhaps, that should be carefully stored away,' but all I could hear, even without her saying anything at all, were the cracks in the old china of her womb, I heard from her eyes the lacerating cries of a mother in labor, I felt her fruit drying with my hot breath, but I couldn't do anything, perhaps I could have said something, my eyes were dark, but even so it would have been possible for me to say, for example, 'Mother, you and I began to demolish this house, the time has come to throw everything out of the larder window, with all the plates and flies, scrape the wood, shake the foundations, make the vigorous walls vibrate, and, with our bluster, make the roof tiles and our flurrying feathers tumble, like falling leaves'; it would have been possible for me to say, 'Let us chip away the bloodstains from our stones with gentle hands, let us add wailing to this rite, the broken lament of the wooden shaker over in the chapel isn't enough'; it would have been possible, but I've already told you, Pedro, my eyes were darker than they'd ever been before, how could I take up the hammer and saw and rebuild the silence of the house and its corridors? But don't misunderstand me, Pedro, even though my eyes were dark, I, the wayward son, the cause of so much suspicion and fear throughout the family, never dreamt of roads, it never crossed my mind to leave home, it had never occurred to me to travel great distances in search of sensual thrills; understand this, Pedro, from the very beginning of my puberty I knew how much disappointment awaited me beyond the limits of our home," I told him, almost drowning in this certainty, taking a deep breath of the spirit of the wine, trying to pull myself together, and between insatiable swigs, I staggered over to a tall, cautious armoire and brought down a box, which I immediately set down near my brother, by that time lost in the hothouse atmosphere of my room, which made the brownish shades of his contemplative gaze drop to the floor, and when I startled him in mid-gesture by opening the box, I thought of saying feverishly, "Pedro, Pedro, what I need now is your silence, lift those blinds, expose your eyes, give them free rein, but restrain from exercising the characteristic family strength and caution, and curb the harsh impetus of your tongue, for I shall only

revive in your damp silence, only to the accompaniment of
that elusive concert, so moisten your lips, mouth and rot-
ting teeth, along with that probe dipping into the pit of your
stomach, fill the leather bag held in by your belt, allow the
wine to seep out through your pores, for it's the only way to
idolize the obscene," is what I meant to say with the voluptuousness of a women's garter collector, but I ended up saying nothing at all, nor did he, as he abruptly checked his
vague gesture, and when I saw my brother nearly finish off
his full glass in one large gulp, I thought of saying, "Oh,
brother, we're beginning to understand each other, since I
can now see your mouth unclogging and, in your eyes, the
sweet effect of the wine stimulating the flow of the blue
milk spurting from your pupils, the same poisonous milk
that at one time irrigated swollen, cancerous nipples," but
there was no point in admonishing him in that rundown
room of mine, the two of us were almost sloshed already,
stuffed with grapes, our damp eyes, our glassy beads assidu-
ously glued to the box I'd flipped over, and in so doing, had
turned over time itself, going back to the surreptitious
nights when I would sneak my burning wrath away from the
fazenda, when I would exchange my soft bed at home for
the hard road leading to the village, disregarding the wandering nocturnal superstitions along that short route, my
flames frightening off both the silent roadside cross and the
shady stories barely concealed behind the iron bars of the

cemetery gate I would pass, encouraged and steadily strengthened on my outing by my profane adolescent thoughts, "Go ahead, Pedro, feel the weight of this most vile object," I said, handing him a tacky piece of thin purple velvet ribbon, a choker necklace; "this remnant, given to me by my first prostitute, is no more than the unfolding, the subtle prolongation of her sulfurous fingernails, the same nails that scratched my back, exalting my yielding skin, sweet paws running over my most intimate parts, 'It's a crazy shame to see this quivering boy, with such a pure face and such a clean body,' she said to me, 'it's a crazy shame to see a boy with peach fuzz like yours, with a smooth, bare chest, burning in bed like kindling; take what you want from me, keep this grimy little ribbon with you and come back to your nook, little saint,' she said caressingly, laughing and whispering luridly, but that is where I used to go, Pedro, that's where I went when I slipped away from the *fazenda* on the hottest nights, to bathe in that insolent faith, I would take communion almost in my sleep, hiding myself from the gentlemen customers, and from the confident ease of all the other boys that also went there, I was awkward in the slimy comfort of those houses and would hide my white feet, clean nails, chalk teeth, neat clothing and smooth, childish face in shame; oh, brother, didn't I lie down on the blazing tangerine earth, in that drosophila-infested kingdom, didn't I surrender like a young boy to that orgy of assassin berries? And wasn't it perchance a precarious peace, the peace that befell me as my body was stretched out on a mattress of poison weeds? Wasn't it perchance temporary, that other slumber wherein my fingernails were dirty, my feet, numb, lice cut trails through my hair and my armpits were visited by ants? Wasn't this second slumber perchance temporary, my head crowned with butterflies, fat larvae escaping my belly button, my cold forehead covered with insects, and my inert mouth kissing scarabs? Such drowsiness, such a stupor, such a nightmare of an adolescence! What rock is this, after all, that weighs so heavily on my body? There is a mysterious chill in this fire; where will I be taken, one day? Such white stone, such anemic dust, such a silent field, such lilies, such tall cypress trees, such long laments, so many ringing wails tolling away at my adolescent body! Very often, Pedro, very often I used to say that there is a funereal silence in everything that goes on, a virtuous alchemy in this unusual mixture, how can this movement be so restful? Often I thought that I should not think at all, that I had already had my fill of this business of thinking, floundering in the saintly witchcraft of the infinite, that's why I often thought I shouldn't take the pensive route, that this should not be my chosen vice in the scheme of things, that I should at most, lay my head down on a pillow of foam, lean back on a mat of leaves, close my eyes and let myself flow with the current, my busy hands skimming aimlessly through algae forests, through floating excrement and thick mud; but every once in a while I would allow myself to escape frivolously from this sleep and ask myself, where will I be taken one day? Pedro, my brother, feast your eyes on these buried memories, on these purple mysteries, on the most playful collection from this dark well: these wilted cloth flowers, this crumpled orchid, this pair of pink garters, this bracelet, these baubles, on all of these trinkets that I always paid for with change stolen from Father; come hither into these objects that lulled me to sleep, saved only so that I could spread them out one day, objects kept buried away in this box so that one day I might dig down and spread them all over the dirt and think to myself, looking back, it was a long, long, but a very long adolescence! Pedro, Pedro the blots in my eyes led me to those denigrated houses, by restoring myself there I could rid myself of my venom, this obscure slime, this excessively panted-after, feebly blasted yolk, but I never once, spying persistently through the doors and windows, I never once, peering through the beaded curtains and red glow of the lamps, caught sight of the salt, the Host, the love of our cathedral! Take this with you, Pedro," I screamed, "take all these scraps home and, tempered with looks of astonishment, tell them how you pieced together the story of the son, the story of the brother; then place an order for a very warm night, or simply a very full moon; spread aromas throughout the yard, create aphrodisiac balms; then assemble our sisters, have them dress up in revealing muslins, and have them wear strappy sandals on their feet; paint their placid cheeks in crimson, their eyelids in green, and their lashes in dark charcoal; adorn their pale, misty arms, their bare necks and their pious fingers, place a few of these simple beads on those ivory statues; see to it that the most subtle of earrings nibble at their earlobes and that carefully designed supports stimulate their breasts; and don't forget their gestures, have them develop a languorous carriage, lay open their cleavage, expose portions of their thighs, create fatal fetishes for their ankles; revolutionize the mechanics of the body, have thick, pestilent bodily fluids flow from those newly red, debauched lips; take these gifts with you and when you get there, announce solemnly, 'From the beloved brother for his sisters,' and say, this is important, say, 'Be very careful, very careful in taking these things out of the bag, for, along with the presents, in payment for Father's sermons, our wayward brother also sends heavy, scornful laughter,' come on, Pedro, put it in the bag," I screamed in gratified rage, witnessing the sudden change coming over him, a rust-red spark flashing through his eyes, his hand flailing through the air frighteningly, the same hand that had been so confident, so prepared to succeed our father's hand, but all at once everything went blank, suddenly I felt his eyes shattering, my brother was discreetly lamenting my dementia, far from realizing that thus perceived I was twice blessed: before I'd journeyed only halfway into lucid darkness, but now I was fully liberated in my insanity; I wanted to tell him: "Temper that hand with a strong voice, restrained tenderness and the right words, run it caressingly through my hair, protect my neck, under these circumstances, this is what Father would do, severely'; it also occurred to me, as I refilled our glasses, that I could aptly encourage him by saying, for example, "Dilate your pupils, set your eyes agog, take my hand in yours, brother, and let's go."

12

(. . . AS I DISCERN the family's utensils and wardrobe inside that trench, I hear diffused, lost voices, but even so, the transparent water that still gushes from the bottom comes as no surprise; I withdraw into our weariness, into so much exhausting struggle, and from this bundle of routines, one by one, I draw out the sublime bones of our code of manners: all excess forbidden, determination required, and constant speeches decrying waste, condemning it as vice, and ever denouncing it as gravely threatening to our work; I meet up again with the tepid messages conveyed by stern looks and eyebrows, and our most hidden chagrins betrayed through our burning cheeks, and the acid agony of the ensuing, sometimes naked reprimands, and also, the crafts school for boys, extolled as the answer to the store-bought goods we should be making with our own hands, and the even more rigid law proclaiming all of our bread should be worked on the *fazenda*: we never ate one morsel of bread that was not homemade, and three times a day, as we broke bread, we concluded our ritual of austerity, and it was also at the table, more than anywhere else that, with our heads bowed, we had our lessons in justice.)

13

ONCE UPON A time, there was a starving man. One day, walking by an unusually large dwelling, he asked the people gathered on the front steps who owned the palace. The king of all peoples, the most powerful man in the universe, they answered. The starving man then approached one of the guards posted at the palace gates and asked for alms in the name of God. "Where are you from?" the guards asked. "Don't you know that all you have to do is appear before our lord and master to have everything you desire?" Encouraged by the response, the starving man, although still somewhat cautious, went through the gates, crossed the spacious patio beyond the entrance, as well as the garden shaded by flourishing trees, and soon he reached the inside of the palace, where he walked through room after room, all of them very large, with tall ceilings but with no furniture whatsoever; managing to find his way through the labyrinth of that strange dwelling, he ended up arriving in a big room covered

in flower- and leaf-decorated tiles, which matched pleas-
antly with the enormous alabaster vase in the middle of the
salon spouting fresh, sweetly murmuring water; a velvet
carpet embroidered with arabesques covered part of the
room where, leaning against some pillows, there was seated
an old man with a soft white beard, his face alight with a
gentle smile. The starving man approached the old man
with the handsome beard, greeting him, "May peace be with
you!" "And with you, peace, and God's mercy and blessing!"
answered the old man, leaning slightly forward. "What do
you desire, poor man?" "Oh, my lord and master, I ask you
for alms in the name of God, for I am so needy I may soon
keel over from hunger." "Oh my God!" exclaimed the old
man. "Is it possible I find myself in a city where a person can
be as hungry as you claim to be? This is intolerable!" "May
God bless you and blessed be your saintly mother," said the
starving man in recognition of the sentiments expressed by
the old man. "Stay here, poor man, I want to break bread
with you and have you serve yourself from the salt of my table." The old man then clapped his hands and ordered a
young servant boy to bring a jug and a basin. Soon afterward,
he said to the starving man: "Guest and friend, come over
here and wash your hands." Then the old man himself stood
up, leaned over the basin and began to rub his hands together grandly under the water supposedly flowing from the
invisible jug. The starving man didn't know what to make of

the scene before his eyes and, since the old man insisted, he took two steps forward and also pretended to wash his hands. "Set the table! Hurry up!" the old man ordered the servants, "and don't take too long with our food, this poor man is almost fainting from hunger." Several servants began to come and go, as if they were setting the table with a cloth and many dishes. The starving man, doubled over in pain, thought to himself: the poor have to be extremely patient with the whims of the powerful, and he abstained therefore from showing any sign of irritation. "Sit here next to me," said the old man. "And honor me with your presence at my table." "I hear and I obey," said the starving man, sitting down on the carpet next to the old man, before the imaginary table. "To my guest, sir, my house is your house and my table is your table. Make yourself at home and eat until you have satisfied your hunger." And since the old man encouraged him to join him, the starving man wasted no time and shortly feigned to eat from the supposed plates, to help himself with his fork to hearty chunks of food, and, moving his chin, to chew and swallow the nonexistent meal. "What do you think of this bread?" asked the old man. "This bread is very pure and good, I've never tasted bread like this before in my life," the starving man answered promptly, without exaggerating his praise. "What a fine guest you are, sir. You make me very happy! But I don't think I deserve so many compliments, otherwise what will you say about the delicacies on your left, this roasted meat, stuffed with rice and almonds, this fish in sesame sauce, or these lamb chops! And what do you think of the aroma?" "The aroma is as inebriating as the presentation and the flavor are divine." "I cannot but acknowledge, honorable guest, that you are extremely indulgent regarding my table, and for this very reason, you will now taste an incomparable morsel from my own hand," said the old man, pretending to take a morsel of food from the platter with his fingers and lifting it to the starving man's lips, saying, "You must chew carefully!" The starving man puckered his lips so that the morsel could be put in his mouth, and then chewed it thoroughly, closing his eyes with pleasure to lend more credence to his performance. "Excellent!" he exclaimed upon finishing. "My dear guest, from your manner of speaking, I can see that you are a man of taste, accustomed to eating at the tables of the great and royal; eat some more, and may you enjoy it." "I'm satisfied, I've already partaken of all of the dishes, I cannot eat any more," said the starving man, smiling in gratitude, and barely containing the pangs of his terrible hunger. The old man clapped his hands and when the servants arrived, he said, "You many bring the dessert." The young servants bustled about, waving their arms in specific gestures and with certain timing, following with other rapid, precise movements indicating that they were removing one tablecloth and spreading another, even though nothing at all had been changed. Finally, the old man

lifted his hand and they withdrew. "Let us sweeten ourselves," said the old man, somewhat pretentiously. "Let us
partake of dessert: this pie, bulging with nuts and pomegranates, with a sort of epic air about it, looks very tempting.
Try some, dear guest, for it has been cut in your honor. Here
is some musk-flavored syrup, perhaps you would like to
pour it over your pie ... Please eat, eat, do not stand on cere-
mony." And the old man set the example, devouring spoonful upon spoonful, with appetite and finesse, in a perfect
performance as if he were savoring real pie. The starving
man imitated him skillfully, even though his hunger pangs
were worse than ever. "Jellies? Fruit? Here are some dried
dates, dates in liqueur, raisins ... What do you prefer? I prefer dried fruit to candied fruit, it still has its natural flavor.
You must also try these figs, fresh off the tree. No? How
about some peaches? Perhaps you prefer plums ... We have
some here, eat up, eat up, God is merciful to all!" And the
starving man, whose mouth, tongue and jaw were tired from
pretending to chew, while his stomach cried out ever more
loudly, answered the old man's persistent comments, "I'm
satisfied, sir, I couldn't possibly eat another thing!" "That is
extraordinary! Considering how hungry you were when you
arrived here, dear guest, it is amazing that you have been so
quickly satisfied; at any rate, it has been an honor to share my
table with you. But we still have not drunk together ..." said
the old man, with a slight trace of mockery on his lips. He

soon clapped his hands and at this signal, several adoles-
cents, their graceful arms showing through light tunics,
came to his aid. They simulated the changing of the tablecloth and the setting of all kinds of glasses and cups upon the
table. The host, still carrying on his performance, filled the
glasses, offering one to the starving man, who, with this per-
mission, took it amiably and lifted it to his lips. "What sublime wine!" he exclaimed, once again closing his eyes and
smacking his lips. And more wine was poured into the
glasses, and other supposed wines were brought, of all types
and flavors. They alternated taking drinks, surrendering to
the unsteady game of the inebriated, slowly swaying their
heads and slumping, in addition to engaging in many other
antics, until all of the bottles had been tasted. And after having poured so much wine into the glasses, the old man
abruptly interrupted the feigned drinking spree, and returning to his former simplicity, his facial expression suddenly
austere, he spoke soberly to the starving man with whom he
had shared the imaginary meal. "Finally, after having
searched the world over, I have found a man of strong spirit,
firm character and who, above all, has proven to have the
most important virtue known to man: patience. For your
rare qualities, from now on, you will live in this house, which
is so huge and so uninhabited, and you can be certain that
you will never lack food on your table." In that very instant,
the servants brought bread, true, robust bread, and the

starving man, thanks to his patience, never knew hunger again.

(How could a man with bread, meat and wine on his table, and salt for seasoning, tell a story about hunger? How could Father, Pedro, have left out so much every time he told that oriental tale? The meeting between the old man and the starving man always ended confusedly, but Father should have told the oft-repeated story of his sermons making use of that therapeutic confusion; the most powerful sovereign in the universe was about to confess that he had, in fact, after much searching, just found a man of strong spirit and firm character and above all, that man had proven himself to have the rarest of all qualities known: patience; but before the compliment could be made, the starving man, with the surprising and unusual strength born of hunger, struck the old man with the handsome white beard violently, explaining himself before the old man's fury, "My lord, master of my laurels, you know very well that I am your submissive slave, the man you have invited to sit at your table, and on whom you have bestowed a banquet of the finest delicacies fit for the greatest king, and to finish off, whose thirst you have quenched with numerous old wines. What more can you expect, my lord, for the spirit of the wine has gone to my head, I therefore am not responsible for raising my fist against my benefactor.')

14

I SWUNG AGILELY over the slab of stone weighing me
down, at first my eyes were stunned, wide open and frozen,
the eyes of a lizard that has recently abandoned immense
waters and slid on to solid rock; I closed my lizard-skin eyelids to protect myself from the light burning into me, and
my word gave way to the world: moss, mud and mire; and
my first thought was in relation to space, and my first saliva
was distinguished by the use of time; all space exists for
journeying, I started saying, to express what I had never before even suspected, that space doesn't exist unless it's fertil-
ized, like when someone goes into virgin forest and stays
there overnight, like when someone penetrates a circle of
people instead of circling it timidly from afar; and in naive,
feverish clarity, I suddenly saw myself in the swift flight of a
white bird, spying between succulent leaves and occupying
new space every second; for the first time, I felt the stream

of life, its strong fishlike odor, and this soaring bird traced a bold, white line inside my thoughts, from inertia to eternal movement; and just as I was emerging from my slumber water, already feeling strong hooves galloping in my chest, I said, blinded by bright lights, I'm seventeen years old and in perfect health and on this rock I am now founding my own church, a church for my own purposes, the church I will attend with my bare feet and bare body, naked, as I came into the world, and there was so much happening to me that all at once I felt I was the prophet of my own history, not a prophet looking upward, but a prophet looking around confidently at the fruit of the earth; and I thought about it and standing there on that rock I said, all of a sudden I know I want, and I know I can!

I watched the sun filling with its ancient blood, tightening its perfect muscles, lancing copper darts into the atmosphere, immediately followed by hot gusts of wind blustering through my ears, prowling around my quiet, plantlike slumber, tangling up the silence of my nest, pecking at my hide with the points of its metallic lights, flinging me into sudden, burning insomnia; boils covered my pores, currents traversed my sleep as I thundered after a graceful doe, each word was a dry leaf and as I raced, I trampled upon the pages of many books, gathering deadly, sour food from among the twigs, so many women, and so many males, so many ancestors, so much accumulated pestilence, what thick syrups run from the fruit of this family! I had simply forged my fist toward the sky and decreed the time had come: impatience also has rights!

15

(I WRITE THIS in memory of my grandfather: in response to the sun, rain and wind, as well as to the other signs of nature that either destroyed our fields or caused them to thrive, he would say (as opposed to our father's indiscriminate insights, which contained grafts from various geographical locations)—with a coarse belch worth all of the sciences, all of the churches and all of our father's sermons: "Maktub."*)

---

* "It is written."

16

RUSTLING RED LEAVES, hundreds of wizards descended from the tallest branches in caravan, riding the wind, shaking amulets in their manes, machinating dark plans out of auditory nettles, and boasting an arsenal of poisonous thorns in open collusion with nature deemed malevolent, they filled the atmosphere with resins and ointments, replenishing our primitive odors, rubbing our obscene noses with the dust of our own pollens and the smell of our clandestine greases, carving out a morbid, fatal appetite inside our bodies; sensing two enormous hands beneath my steps, I hid myself away in the old house of the *fazenda*, made of it my refuge, the playful hiding place of my sleeplessness and its pain; I locked away the darkest parts of my libido there between the pages of a prayer book, I moved around the house among gray rats, returning the roots of my feet to their origins, exploring the silence of the halls, investigating the creaking wood, the cracks in the walls, the slack windows, the darkness of the kitchen and, inflating my nostrils to absorb the family's most distant atmosphere, I relived the squalid whispers and spiderwebs dangling from the rafters, the peaceful history leaning over the windowsills, and the stronger history in the beams; the only thing breaking into the damp silence of the well was an arm of sunlight reaching slyly through the cracked tiled roof, lighting a small flame, cold and porous, on the wood floor; with my sacred, profane torment in every corner, I filled the deserted rooms with my pleas, and lit the infamously frightening, esoteric shadows in the old house with my fire and faith; and as the underground creaking seeped up at me through the floorboards, I kept saying, as if in prayer, I'll burn this wood, these bricks and mortar yet, then I'll transform the largest room in this house into a barn for my testicles (such fertile earth and so much lamentation, such restless shoots bursting from these seeds!), I was spilling all my blood along that atavistic trail, resting my reborn fetus in the hay, lulling it with my hands, and scattering the premature petals of a white rose, I was already rushing through the waiting period, taking off in a drunken state (such lucid wine filled my eyelids!), and spying through the cracks like an animal, my presence in the old house sending signals through the mirror of my eyes, like the intermittent, jagged steel we used to use in the woods or pastures to send out our forbidden messages: such anticipated passion, such pestilence, such crying out!

17

TIME, TIME IS versatile, time works mischievously, time would play with me, time would stretch out provokingly, it was a time filled only with waiting, keeping me in the old house for days on end; it was also a nerve-wracking time, of muddled sounds, confusing my antennae, making me hear imaginary allurements clearly, awakening me to the weight of a harsher sentence: I am crazy! And the saliva of this word was so corrosive, caressing me in desperate fantasies, forming terrible masks over my face, occasionally, tossing me gently into the affectionate initiations of religious orgy: a colt ran through the fields with all its tack, scraping our bloody barbed-wire fences, guiding me to the enchanted orchard cove! Such virulent pulp stored amidst the silver leaves, staining my teeth, inflaming my tongue, blotching my adolescent skin! Time, time, time studied me calmly, time punished me, I heard the steps on the small front staircase clearly and distinctly: such a sudden shock, how upsetting to see my heart leap out at me unexpectedly like an injured bird, shrieking and jumping in the palm of my hand! I rushed toward the door: no one was there; I searched the dried shrubbery in the abandoned garden, but nothing moved, there was a silence-filled, still wind, not even the most timid heartbeat traversed the fields, there's a limit to the imagination I could still reason, there was a time when nothing went wrong! I returned to the room I used to stay in, flying directly over to the window, peering through the slit (God!): she was there, not far from the house, beneath the old washboard shed, partially hidden by the old bougainvillea branches, shying away after her bold advance, and then watching my window distrustfully, barefoot with her country-girl figure and her gracefully disheveled clothing, white, white, her face so white, and I was reminded of doves, the doves of my childhood, and I also saw myself peeking from behind the blinds, as I used to peek, huddled in a corner of the barn, from where I would spy on the fearful, aloof dove as it measured its own movements distrustfully, its meticulous, precise beak pecking back and forth, advancing steadily along the trail of kernels, and I would spy and wait, because there is a time for waiting and a time to be agile (that is a science I learned as a child and later forgot); that's the reason I would follow it and, in my imagination, read the crooked, graceful little crosses imprinted in the dirt by its soft feet as it advanced and withdrew; and there was a time to be agile, then there was an abrupt rustling of wings as the wire netting closed over it surreptitiously, my hands quickly forming a nest, I soon held but a quiver between my fingers as I ran through the yard in turmoil calling out, "It's mine, it's mine, it's mine," stopping only to look more carefully at its small, round eyes—shrewd, but by then only out of frightened panic, and I would determinedly pluck the feathers from its wings, temporarily curtailing its extensive flight—there would be a time for new feathers and new wings, and also for new love, and that was the sweet imprisonment awaiting it upon its once again taking full flight; the doves in my yard could fly away freely, they took long journeys, but always returned, because I had nothing but love for them and wanted nothing else from them, and when they flew far, far away I would recognize them on the most distant rooftops among the uninitiated flocks whom I also hoped to bring into my immense garden some day; she was there, white, white, her face so white and I could sense all her doubt, confusion and pain, and because I was so filled with faith, I believed I couldn't possibly be mistaken in my burning, my passion and delirium; I began imagining how I should have drawn her in, with a winding trail of grapes leading to the front stairs, and bunches of fresh pomegranates draped in the front windows, and vibrant-colored garlands entwined in the old railing of the big veranda surrounding the house;

there was a time for waiting, but I was already stumbling, turning impatiently from the window, I violently kicked the straw I had collected little by little and built up day by day in the middle of the room; a gusty dust pile blew through my head, and for a minute, I was lost in that whirlwind, contemplating confusedly the disturbance in my own nest: there was life in the room! I went back to peeking through the slit in the window; she was no longer inside the shed and I was no longer inside myself, I had flown to the front door: time, time, this sometimes gentle, sometimes cruel tormentor, the absolute devil qualifying everything, deciding everything to this day and for ever—which is why I bow to it fearfully, held in suspense, wondering when, when exactly is the precise moment of crossing over? Which instant, which terrible instant marks the leap? Which gale and spatial depth conspire, toying with the limit? The limit where all newly vibrationless things no longer simply make up life in the day-to-day current, but have become life in the subterraneous memory; she then stood before me in the entrance, white, white, her face so white, filtering the ancient colors of extremely different emotions, composing in the door frame the picture I still don't know where to hang, in the rush of life or in the current of death; and there we stood facing each other motionlessly, silently, our minds in a blind knot, yet she had only to cross the threshold and it became no more than a boy's science, nonetheless, already a science made up of instants, a piece of string in one hand and my heart in the other, agility was impossible knowing the moments of patience that awaited me, any tumble would be premature, harming the bird, causing tumultuous, injured flight; kernel by kernel, second by second, as the dove approached the wire-net trap, it became more cunning, pecking firmly at the dirt, but with a trembling neck, like the indecisive arm of a water mill, midway to its destiny; with each peck and poke, it would shake its wings, threatening with its feathers to back away until, crossing over the arc-shaped frame, a sweet treat would obliterate the wire netting stretched out on the dirt; it was a boy's science, but it was a complex science, one kernel too many, or one second less and the bird might become dispirited with excess or with longing, there was just the right, calculated amount, the amount that would maintain the dove's trust once caught; in one hand, a flaming heart, and in the other, the agile string, just waiting to be geometrically tightened, swiftly tracing over the industrious calculations in the sand; no rapture, no jerking while pulling the string, not one extra second in the weight of the tense arm.

18

AND THIS WAS the second: she crossed the threshold, passing me by as if I were a log placed upright before her, impassive, dry and highly inflammable; I didn't move, a tense block of wood, although I could feel her demented steps behind me and was imagining a dark resin obscuring her eyes, but gradually, the indecisive shadow began to trace bold movements, suddenly losing itself inside the hallway tunnel: I closed the door, I had pulled the string, knowing that somewhere in the house, she would find herself in absolute stillness, her slackened wings flattened beneath the powerful weight of destiny; I took my shoes and socks off right there by the front door, and as I felt my bare feet on the damp wood floor, I also felt my body suddenly obscene, a bone emerging virulently from my flesh, there were spurs on my ankles, what a sanguine crest, such vast passion, expectant shivering! I delved into the hallway, stepping on a dangerous runner, a mild tremor shaking my entire body, yet

I walked without making a sound, not one splinter, not one creak, I soon paused at just the right place, it was written: she was there, lying in the straw, her arms at her sides, she could have reached the sky through the window, but her eyes were closed, like those of a corpse, and I still ask myself how I rallied my strength to mount that galloping risk, my flaring back was up and there was a pile of dried straw at my feet, but in a split second no one ever questions the destiny of their own actions, I had only to know for sure, the passing second passes definitively, and in a whirl I lay down burning next to her, launching myself entirely, like an arrow, a poison-tipped rod, and finally, enveloping in my arms the decision to postpone life no longer, I gripped her hand boldly, but the hand I held tightly in mine was limp, there was no word in that palm, no quivering, no soul in that wing, I was holding a dead bird in my hand, and finding myself thus suddenly lost, not knowing which byway was mine, nor that of my faith, the two of us one and the same until then, I watched fearfully as my continent split; what a precarious separation, how uncertain, how many hands and clumps of hair, I ended up yelling out my own part deliriously, praying as I had never ever done before, bringing forth a strange, ringing plea from my feverish lips, "A miracle, a miracle, my God," I begged, "a miracle and in my lack of faith I will bring back Your existence, let me live this singular passion," I pleaded as the wild flesh of my fingers tried to revitalize the cold flesh of hers, "let this hand breathe with mine, oh God, and in payment for this breath of air, I will soar, lying tenderly over Your body, and with my capable fingers I will remove the golden hook that long ago speared Your mouth, and then I'll scrupulously cleanse Your wounded face, carefully removing the webs covering the ancient light in Your eyes; I will not forget Your sublime nostrils, they'll be so clear, You will breathe unknowingly; I will also remove the corrupt dust suffocating Your terrestrial hair, and zealously remove the lice that have left tracks in Your scalp; I'll clean Your dark fingernails with mine, and will eliminate, one by one, the dragonflies laying eggs in Your pubis, I'll wash Your feet in blue lavender water and, with my loving eyes, anxiously mend the open wounds between Your toes; I'll also blow hot air from my own lungs into You, and when Your veins run thin, then You will find Your ragged, fine skin filled with sugar and Your mouth, hardened and agape, transformed into ripened fruit; and soft fuzz will gracefully replace the old hair on Your body, as well as the rank growth in Your armpits, and new, soft curls will grow over the plane of Your pubis, and fine baby down will grow along the sweet halo of Your ever-tumid burgundy anus; and this resurgence will occur in an adolescent body through the same miracle as the appearance of silky-smooth feathers on molting birds and the new, sparkling foliage on blossoming trees in springtime; then, in a rejoicing, elegant sweep, a gentle wind will once again lend

Your hair its lofty mien; I will then dress You in a white satin robe with a large gold-braid-trimmed yoke, and place stone rings containing all the prophets' gazes on Your fingers, iron bracelets on Your wrists, and olive branches on Your noble head; sylvan resins will coat Your fresh, clean body, and clusters of stars will cover Your boy's head as if You were riding on a litter of lilies; and You will be served delicacies on grapevine leaves, and also fresh grapes, oranges and pomegranates, and from more distant orchards, reaped from my parents' memories, dried fruit, figs, and date honey; then Your glory will be more magnificent than it has ever been throughout Your entire history! But now I feel such doubt and ambiguity in this hand, there must be a soul throbbing somewhere in this feeble plaster, perhaps a breath, or a future scar, a premonitory memory of this pain, a miracle, my God, and I will bring You back to life and in Your name, I will sacrifice a rigorous, agile wild animal from among my father's herd, one of the young, dewy lambs out grazing during the bluish early morning hours; I'll flex up my arms, then tie up its tender paws, two by two, with knife and rope, immobilizing the frightened beast under my feet; with my left hand I'll grasp its still button-like horns and gently twist its head around to the pure back of the neck, while with my right, I'll deliberately strike the blow, splitting its throat, liberating its bleating along with a dark violent rush of thick blood; I will then take the quivering lamb in my arms and hang it upside down from a pole, and the dense blood still running from the severed tubes will flow out onto the ground; I will pierce its hide with a determined reed, strong and resistant enough so that I can, as my uncle used to do on his flute, blow and fill the beast with an ancient, desperate song, inflating it, as only an animal three days gone will inflate; and once skinned, its belly torn open from one end to the other, there will be the intimacy of hands and entrails, blood and virtue, enticement and maxims, of exasperated candles weeping sacred oils and many other waters, so that Your obscene hunger is also revitalized; a miracle, a miracle," I was still pleading, inflamed, when all at once I began to feel the anemic hand I was holding had become the small, warm, fleeting heart of a bird, a crazed red word now moving in my palm! Shivering and blinded from those whitewashed walls, I rubbed the water from my eyes and said, still feverish, "God exists, and in Your name I will sacrifice an animal that we may be provided with roasted meat, decant several intoxicating wines that we may become drunk like two boys, and climb steep hills in our bare feet (a stampede of angels, the strumming of zithers, I can already hear the chiming of bells!), and holding hands, together we will set the world on fire!"

19

"ANA, PEDRO, IT was Ana, my hunger was for Ana," I suddenly exploded in a peak, expelling in one isolated, violent
jet the hardened core of my ripe, pestilent boil, "Ana was my
illness, she was my insanity, my air, my splinter and chill, my
breath, the impertinent insistence in my testicles," I yelled
with my mouth wide open, exposing the texture of my raving tongue, ignoring the guardian hidden between my teeth,
spattering clots of blood, releasing the nauseating words that
had been forever locked away in silence, "I was the crazed
brother, the raving brother, the vile-smelling brother, I was
the one with the slime of so many slugs and the devil's slob-
ber coating my skin, ticks in my pores, confused ants in my
armpits, and profuse fruit flies celebrating my filthy body; go
get it quickly, Pedro, hurry up and bring me the washtub in
which we bathed as children, the warm water, the ash soap
and scratchy sponge, the white, fluffy towel; wrap me up inside, wrap me up in your arms, dry my tormented hair, then

run your earnest hand down the back of my neck, hurry and fulfil this tender ritual, it is up to you, Pedro, you opened our mother first, you were the one toasted as the hallowed eldest," I said, foaming and in pain, slipping lasciviously on strange saliva, yet even having fallen into possessed wrath, I was still able to see my brother covering his face with his hands, terrified by the impact of my fury, it was impossible to figure out the cracks in his burnt-brick face, impossible to read the expression of his mouth, to determine which stone spark was, perhaps, shattering his eyes; it was clear he was probing for support, was definitely in search of solid, hard ground, and I could even hear his cries for help, but seeing him in such a profoundly startling, still position (it was my father), it also occurred to me that he might have withdrawn as an exercise in patience, that there in the dark he might be consulting the elders' texts, the noble, ancestral pages, leafing through in search of serenity, but in the current of my trance the blending together of his pain and respect for the writings of the ancients no longer mattered, I had to scream out furiously that there was more wisdom in my madness than in all of Father's wisdom, that my illness suited me better than the health of the family suited them, that my remedies had never been written about in textbooks, but that there was another medicine (mine!), and except for mine, I acknowledged no other science, and that everything was merely a question of perspective, and only my point of view held any meaning whatsoever, and that it was the apposite prerogative of gluttons to test the virtue of patience with other people's hunger, and I said everything spasmodically and obsessively in a verbal rage, and wreaking havoc, I overturned the sermon table, destroying clamps, bolts and moorings; nevertheless, leveling off, aware of the plumb, establishing a different balance, while using all my strength to go steadily beyond, and tightening mainly my clandestine muscles, I was soon to rediscover everything animalistic about myself, my hooves, jaws and spurs, and an oily grease coated my sculptured self as I galloped, my feathered mane flying behind me, my Sagittarius paws denting the soft belly of the world and, consuming a grain of wheat along with a fat slice of wine-soaked wrath in this pasture, I, the epileptic, the possessed, the crazed, I, who was starved, summoned into my convulsive speech the soul of a flame, a veronica cloth, and a spattering of mud, then I mixed into this flowing broth the spicy name of our sister, the perverted name of Ana, and removing the nectar of my dagger from the fringes of these tender words, embarked passionately with my quivering flesh into urgent confessional voluptuousness (such shivering, so many suns, such agony!), until all at once, my limp body dropped sweetly from exhaustion.

20

I FOUND PEACE as I lay in the hay, naked as the day I was
born; the room was dark, it was perhaps the time of day
when mothers rock their children to sleep, blowing gentle
fantasies into their ears; yet outside it was still daylight, a
mild evening, the gentle sky entirely composed of a languishing, dubious pink hue; I fell into thought at this peaceful hour, when cows roam in search of water, and the last of
the evening's birds seek their resting place; and I also
thought how, if I were to lean over the windowsill, I could
watch frayed clouds shifting patiently like an old man's
beard until a gentle dark dome in the sky would put out the
day, and then gradually the dome would become covered
with nipples for nurturing little pajama-clad children during the early morning hours; and I could foresee that upon
awakening I would feel two enormous hands beneath my
steps, nature engulfing me and making me her own, opening her fat arms and spraying me with fresh dew, rolling me

up inside a blanket of grass, and taking me to her breast like
a child; she would quell my fears earnestly, hurrying to light
the dawn, and in the morning, she would dissipate the still-
distant smoke, her hair blowing through profuse winds
would dry my feet, and my own misty eyelashes would
cleanse my eyes; then a vague, yet vast touch would run
over my peaceful body, tickling me softly, ruffling my tender
hair caressingly, sprinkling my young flesh with talcum
powder, and hanging around my neck a red string, dangling
an enchanted, fist-shaped bone amulet to ward off evil and
illness; and over in a joyous spot in the woods, below full,
leafy trees, where the earth plays its game of shadows and
light, there would be fresh, flowing water and rippling
creeks nearby and new, green leaves adorning my head,
thickets in my teeth would freshen my breath, and honey
and pomegranates would await me, ageless doves would
rest on my shoulders, and on the atmosphere's immense
breast, a yellow ball would balance, wildly caressing my lips;
and of course, Ana was there next to me, her presence so
certain, so necessary that, in the dim hours of nightfall, I
thought of leaving the old house and going outside to the
deserted garden and reaching up and pulling at a shrub
branch to pick an ancient flower for her knees; instead, with
clumsy, peasant hands, frightening two timid lambs hidden
away in her thighs, I slowly touched her humus-coated
belly, felt the terrain, designed a flower bed, tilled the earth,

and sowed petunias in her belly button; I also sensed my
urethra, a chrysanthemum stem released, and thought how
often we would be able to laugh riotously like two children
spraying each other with urine, wetting our bodies as we
had done just a while ago, ever exchanging each other's saliva with our nimble tongues, sticking our faces together by
way of our tear-dampened cheeks, thinking only that we
were made of earth and that everything inside of us would
germinate solely with each other's waters, the sweat of one
exchanged with the sweat of the other; and in this reverie
of earth and waters, someone gently lowered my eyelids,
leading me unawares into a light slumber; I didn't realize
that love required watching over: there is no such thing as
everlasting peace, no such thing as infinite, supreme good-
ness, nor a goblet without a trace of venom; it was common
knowledge, I had been so frivolous, someone stronger than
I was pulling the string and, clever, smart child that I was, I
had fallen directly into the trap set by destiny: fate had
reached its long arm to take the fruit from deep inside me,
pinched its long, thin fingers into my very depth, and in the
blink of an eye, had suddenly turned my sweet world inside
out; frightened and upset, I groped the hay, and as I opened
my eyes, two burning coals, I was absolutely certain my
body had been carved out to receive the devil himself: as
soon as I realized she was gone, I was overcome with hor-
rendous rage and right away found myself unexpectedly,

somewhat cautiously, in the dark hallway; I spoke out clearly, "If you're in the house, Ana, please answer," it was a sensible, almost mild question, I was trying, although burning up inside, to entice the old house by urging the bat-filled silence and ghosts to take my side, to join me as allies, one and all, and I repeated, "Answer me, Ana," and again my voice reverberated in waves, and I waited expectantly (I had to prove my patience), but since there was no answer, with the company of the creaking wood and my growing furore, I began to search the entire house, room by room, corner by corner, shadow by shadow and, finding not one sign of her, I fled to the veranda, the loneliness of the dark night sending a chill throughout my marrow: the old garden bushes, destroyed by the wild climbers growing everywhere, had been transformed into phantasmagoric masses inhabiting a noisy insect kingdom; leaning over the railing, I looked out in every direction, and way over by the pastures, the cattle, some still standing, formed a silhouette as they slept beneath an old pepper tree; in a lung-bursting cry, I bellowed out for Ana with all my might, but to no avail, the ruins before me in the garden retained their somnolent stillness, and at that time of night, the cattle were like granite, the nature surrounding me was so indifferent and filthy, not one sign of concern for my plight, what a desperate sense of helplessness! Convinced she had run away, I felt like tearing at my face, ripping myself apart with my own

fingernails until I bled, how distressful! I fled barefoot from
the old house as fast as I could, my winged legs leading me
to a clearing further along where, through the narrow arch
of the chapel doorway, I saw—I don't even remember if I
was stunned—someone lighting candles inside; I checked
my flight, but only for a second, after all, there was no reason to stop, I had nothing to reconsider, so I took off once
more and, as I got nearer, I curbed my staggering steps, trying not to fluster her praying with my gasping: Ana was
kneeling there, before the small oratory, and I recognized
the altar cloth covering her hair; she was still fingering the
first beads of the rosary, her eyes lit by two candles as she
stared at the image above her; while watching her pious
profile, her lips in small, tense, rapid movement, for a moment I was overwhelmed with dizziness, but I quickly revived and found myself inside the chapel, which was very
different from what I had known in the bright days of our
childhood; I had stepped into a cramped, bronze chamber
where all my demons were tightly positioned, disguised in
a myriad of shadows, what a show destiny had made of time
(mixing the two of them together!), covering it with planning and industry to delay the finale: before pulling the
string, destiny had made sure the candles were lit, and that
Ana was on her knees, then generously and liberally there
in the chapel, it had left me to choose between the clay
saints and the devil's legions; just as I had done as a boy

with the innocent dove: on the one side, nutritionless sand, on the other, the promise of abundance inside the wire netting; since my childhood I had been no more than a shadow, created in the image of destiny, and I had further complicated matters along the way: even though, hidden beneath the sand, the line determining the outcome was stretched as straight as an arrow, I would make a curving trail of kernels to reach the trap; why all the foolishness, the endless scenes and the gorging with expectations, if my fate had been predetermined? As soon as I stepped inside, I stood over and behind her and I too began to mumble the rosary in an intense murmur, it was the rope I was drawing from my well, knot by knot: "I love you, Ana, I love you, Ana, I love you, Ana," I kept saying in blazing madness, like someone in prayer, someone with dubious intentions, and what ecstasy it was to fondle her back, to trace her vertebrae, to peck the back of her neck with my warm tongue; but my prayers were useless, her back was absolutely motionless, the altar-cloth veil revealed not a single vibration throughout the thick decorative lace running just below her shoulders; even so, I continued, knot by knot, "Ana, listen to me, that's all I'm asking," I said, striving for serenity, I had to prove my patience, to use reason, while making the very best of its versatility, I also needed to bribe the clay saints, the clear stones and the illuminated parts of that chamber to entice and bring the entire chapel over to my side, just as

I had tried to do over in the old house, "What happened between us was a miracle, dear sister, branches from the same trunk, with a common roof, no betrayal, no disloyalty, and the superfluous, yet fundamental certainty of relying on each other both in times of joy and adversity; it was a miracle, dear sister, to have discovered that even our bodies fit together, and that through our union our childhood will endure, with no sorrow over our playthings, no breach in our memories, nor trauma to our shared history; we have discovered a miracle, above all, we have become whole within the confines of our own home, confirming Father's words that happiness is only found in the bosom of the family; it was a miracle, dear sister, and I refuse to be disillusioned over this small stroke of destiny, for I mean to be happy, I, the odd son, the black sheep whose confessions no one will hear, the inveterate ne'er-do-well of the family, yet the one who loves our home, I love this land and I also love the work, contrary to what everyone believes; it was a miracle, dear sister, it was a miracle I'm telling you, and it was a miracle from which there is no return: everything is going to change from here on in, I'm going to rise at the crack of dawn with our brothers, go to work with Father, till the earth and sow the seeds, tend to all the blooming and growth, and share our concerns over the crops, I'm going to pray for rain and sunshine for our fields when water and light are scarce, care for the ripening grapes, participate deservedly in the harvest, bring home the fruit and, with all of this, I'm going to prove that I too can be of use; I have blessed hands for planting, dear sister, I never neglect even one sprout from our seeds, and am very careful when transplanting, I always know what the land needs, how to appease it when necessary, to strengthen it for all types of crops and, although I respect its need for rest, I'll see to it, as Father says, that each and every inch of our land is productive, I know a lot about planting the fields, and I'll also be praiseworthy in looking after our animals, I know how to approach them, gain their trust and their gentle regard, I know how to feed them correctly by preparing the grains according to my own taste and mixing salts into the troughs to strengthen their muscles, and I also know how to weed our pastures to make them thrive, mow the grass to just the right height, and cut the grass at just the right time, to expose it to heat and humidity, and since I'm so skilful with the scythe and pitchfork, I can also cut it for storage in bunches or bales, as needed; I know how to milk cows, I dote on the calves and am kind to the mothers when I take away their young, rinsing the sticky milk from their udders, while preventing the first flow from leaking through my fingers, and always wiping them carefully so they maintain the rich smell of the corrals and stables; I have an enormous store of affection for the entire herd, as well as a clinical eye to spot the yearlings that will someday reproduce, and I know how to remove infectious worms stuck in their hide, all the while forewarning them against iridescent horsefly dreams and rendering their coat smooth, soft and shiny once again; I know how to protect the herd from other stings as well, how to shelter the cows from rough winds, and how to lead them to shady trees at high noon, or under cover during heavy storms, I can also find the best water for quenching their intense thirst since I know all the ponds on the *fazenda*; I love our nanny goats and ewes, and can cuddle timid one-month-old lambs, I have a soft spot for frightened animals, my pastures will be a mixture of rustic flute melodies, flowering grasses and gentle winds rippling through the fields; I have a shepherd's soul, dear sister, I make sure all the species get along, I'm a master, even when it comes to the most suspect crossbreeds, I know how to multiply Father's herd; and along with this vast knowledge, I'll care for all the fowl, our gregarious chickens, the exuberant roosters, the graceful, wobbling teal, the ducks, flat from their beaks to their webbed feet, the puffed-up turkeys, as well as the adventure-seeking, ornery guinea hens, bearing their sickly lump as if it were a crest; I know how to gather eggs from the nests, and how to make certain stray eggs are forever protected under warm brooders, and I never flounder around timid hens laying their chaste eggs into baskets or nests dangerously suspended from the barn beams; I also know how to take care of the watering troughs, maintaining fresh, clear water in the clay containers and keeping them in the shade to prevent contamination, I know all about mangers, too, how to vary the feed with kernels, greens and meal, and with no risk of damaging our vegetables, I'm going to allow free pecking on the fertile land, I can be useful for lots of other things too, making stakes, fixing gates, I'm exacting with the crossbar, I have a carpenter's precise blood running through my veins, and I love the trees as much as I do the wood, I can identify them all by their smell alone and know how to make the best use of the pea tree, the cedar, the pine, the peroba and the calabash; I am going to take over the maintenance of Father's tools, increase his set and clean everything meticulously after each use, removing scraps from the hammer claws, the level vial and the saw teeth, I'll keep them oiled to prevent rusting so they're always ready, for I'm well aware that no one cuts without a blade, that tools not only forge the way to the finished product, they often forge our willpower to do a good job; I am also planning to be the handyman, I'm going to eliminate any moisture dampening our reserve harvest, replace sagging beams, change latches and bolts, I'm going to whitewash wherever needed and carefully build a new shed, and, of course, make certain it's proportional and that the roof tiles are carefully laid, with enough space below the overhang for the swallows; I am very versatile, dear sister, I'm good at so many things, I want to be busy, my arms are just waiting, I want to be called upon whenever there is work to be done, I can hardly stand my own energy, I can accomplish any task under the sun that could possibly need doing on this *fazenda*; and whenever I have free time, I'll turn the soil in the garden beds with good surplus manure, and sprinkle it with chaff, kernels and siftings, so everything will flourish, the flowers surrounding the house, the birds in our trees, the doves on our rooftops and the fruit in our orchards; and every afternoon after working from sunup to sundown, I'll come home and wash the blessed sweat from my body, put on sturdy, clean clothes and at dinner time, when everyone is gathered and the homemade bread has been placed on the tablecloth, I'll share in the sublime sensation of having contributed with my own two hands to provide for the family; contrary to what everyone believes, I know a lot about herds and planting, but I've kept all of this fundamental knowledge to myself, which, if put to good use, would serve the family more than it would me, and I've put up with everyone's scorn without ever letting anyone in on the nature of my idleness, but I am so tired, dear sister, I want to be a part of things, to be with everyone, don't exclude me and don't let my talents go to waste, it's everyone's loss; I can learn even more than I already know, and will always undertake my tasks earnestly, I'm dedicated and thorough in what I do, and I'll do everything with joy, but I need a reason, I need to be compensated for my work, to be sure I can pacify my hunger in this exotic pasture, I need your love, dear sister, I know I'm not asking too much, what I'm asking of you is fair, it's my due, my share, the ration I have coming to me," and pausing in this outpouring of pleas, I waited, lost in confused dreams, my eyes fixed on her back, and my thoughts fixed in a disturbing rut, but it had all been pointless, Ana remained motionless on her knees, her body so wooden I could not even tell whether or not she was breathing; "Ana, listen to me, that's all I ask …" I fell back into the same calm manner, I've already mentioned I was well aware that I needed to prove my patience, to speak to her with reason (and how unabashedly versatile it was!), to use my good sense to sensitize all the saints, I needed the entire chapel to back me up: "Ana, listen to me, I've already said it once, but I'll say it again: I'm so tired, I want to be a part of things, to be with everyone, I, the wayward son, the perpetual convalescent, on whom the suspicion of being an aberrant growth weighs so heavily; I want you to know, dear sister, that I do not rebel by choice, nor do I mean to grimace and scowl all the time, nor to harbor the anger that leaves its harsh traces, nor do I choose to hide myself away, and certainly not to live in this nightmarish state for which I am condemned: I want to change the muddy clay of my mask, dear sister, to eliminate the spark of madness lighting my eyes, to remove their vile shadows from my adolescent face, to wash away for ever this blemish on my forehead, this dreary scar no one sees, but that you all sense; everything is going to change, dear sister, my face will soften, I'll abandon my isolation, my mute silence, I'm going to get along with all my brothers and sisters, make my life a part of theirs, would that I be ever present at the bright table of our family meals; I'm going to speak lightly, like everyone else, make conversation with neighboring farmers, for example, about next year's promising harvest, or mention that we can lend out one of our new breeders, I'll borrow their important manner and finish up by commenting that recent rains have made the crops flourish; when I'm out on the road and meet up with people, I'll tip my hat, just like they do, and in town, when I go to buy salt, wire or kerosene, I'll stop and chat in every store, shake hands, and smile openly at everyone who looks my way; I'll be upright and good, show concern and consideration, I like to help other people, I'm perfectly capable of being friendly, and when I have friends, I won't let them down, I'm going to stop distilling poison at the onset of my loving impulses; and one of these nights after dinner, when shadows have fallen all over the gardens surrounding our house, and quiet darkness has taken over the veranda, when Father, with his grave manner, has become lost in his thoughts, I'm going to approach him, pull up a chair and sit down right next to him, then I'll amaze him even more when I start up very naturally the distant conversation we never had; and as soon as I say, 'Father,' and before I go on, calmly and firmly, I'll sense the barely contained joy in his face shining through the light in his damp eyes, and the thrill of his ideas eagerly falling into place so that he can announce that the son for whom the family has feared is no longer cause for anxiety, that there is no further need to worry over him, and, because the son has spoken, there is no longer any reason to be afraid of him; and after he has listened to everything I have to say as I unravel the concerns of the whole family through our conversation, I can already tell you what our coming together will be like: first he'll take my shoulders in his hands, and have me stand up, as he himself has already done, then he'll take my head between his palms, and look me firmly in the face to rediscover in my features those of his youth, and before I ask for his long-awaited blessing, looking downward, I will feel his rough lips on my forehead as he kisses me austerely right where my scar used to be; and that's how it will be, plus all the other wonderful things that will happen afterward; help me to lose myself in the family's love with your love, dear sister, I can't take one step forward in this darkness, I want to escape this endless night, to be free of this torment, we're always hearing that the sun rises for everyone, so I want my portion of light, my share of this warmth, that's all I need, and as soon as I get it, I'll give you my lucid soul, my illuminated body and my eyes, glowing at last; just to think of it, Ana, my cup runneth over,

I can already feel my muscles strengthening once again, I'm bursting with joy, I could even lift up the world with one arm; and some day of rest, after lunch on a Sunday, when the wine has begun filling our heads with warm words and the sun is dropping from the sky, you and I will go outside to enjoy an exuberant walk; we will cut through the woods and down the cypress-bordered road and as we near the chapel, we'll leave the lament of the beefwoods behind to answer the calls of the coconut palms urging us out into the open pastures, insisting we lay down on the soft belly of the fields; and only when, beneath that ancient sky, we've dyed our teeth in the blood of the mulberries picked along the way, will we surrender completely to the vast, circumspect silence, inhabited at that time of day by mysterious insects, by birds flying high above and by the distant ringing of cow-bells; give me your hand, dear sister, so much awaits us, just reach out to me, that's all I ask of you, everything rides on this one act of yours, my outlook, my behavior, and my vir-tues: kindness and generosity will be the first, and they'll always be with me, I promise you this sincerely with all of my heart and I'll keep this promise with no effort whatso-ever, but everything, everything, Ana, begins with your love, it is the nucleus, the seed, your love for me is the be-ginning of the world," I kept talking insistently, obsessively, making myself believable, although exhausted from my own carrying on, I was disturbed to my very bones! "You must understand, Ana, that Mother gave birth to more than just children when she filled the house, we were soaked in the most sublime syrups from our orchards, rolled in the transparent honey of the honeybees and along with the many aromas rubbed into our skins, we were made dizzy with the delicate blossom water from the orange trees; can we be blamed for this plant called childhood, its seduction, its vigor and earnestness? Can we be blamed if we were sorely hit by the fatal virus of excessive caresses? Can we be blamed for the many tender leaves that hid the morbid stem of these boughs? Can we be blamed if we were the ones to be caught in the netting of this trap? Our fingers, kneecaps, our hands and feet, even our elbows are entangled in this birdlime mesh, you must understand that not only our fingernails and feathers, but our entire bodies would be mutilated if we were to separate; so, help me, dear sister, help me so that I can help you, the same help I can offer you, you can bring to me, understand that when I speak about me, it is the same thing as speaking only about you, understand that our two bodies have forever been inhabited by the same soul; give me your hand, Ana, answer me, say just one word, anything, at least show me a sign in your silence, a slight nod of your head is enough, or a hint with the tips of your shoulders, a gentle motion of your hair, or the soles of your feet, the smallest promise of movement in your arches," I begged, but Ana didn't hear me, the uselessness of everything I was saying was clear, and it was also clear I was using up all my resources for a dubious reason: to keep my soul light, available, how threatening, how dangerous! I advanced three steps forward and stood barefoot before her, leaning against the oratory, my face in the shadows, hers illuminated by candlelight; standing there in the dark, my eyes were very bright and almost clashed with hers looking up at me, but it was unbelievable: Ana was so strong-willed, she didn't even see me; kneeling there, she worked away at her rosary zealously, only fervor, water, and grime coated her cheeks, washed her flesh, cleansed her leprosy, what a purifying bath! "Take pity on me, Ana, take pity on me before it's too late," then, with a more profane approach, I mumbled on, "but try to understand what I mean when I speak to you like this: I'm not attempting to earn your devotion with my pleas, it's more of a signal, it's my warning, I assure you, the clairvoyance of a dark premonition goes along with my appeal: if there's a breach in this passion I won't be pious, I don't have your faith, I'm unable to find your saints when all goes wrong," I said, already hearing the bleating of a lost ewe running through a red meadow, darting out to the valley, and realizing that somewhere a fire was being lit of resinous logs, that it was neither night nor day, but a time that balanced midway, a time that dissolved somewhere between the dog and the wolf: "Ana, we still have time, don't release me with your refusal, do not leave me with so much choice, I don't want to be this free, don't force me to lose myself in the bitter dimensions of this immense space, don't push me away, don't drive me away, don't abandon me at the gateway of this vast trail, I've already said it, and I'll say it once more: I'm tired, I want my place at the family table, urgently! I'm begging you, Ana, and just to remind you, the family can be spared; in this imperfect world, this precarious world, where even the greatest truth can't get beyond the limits of confusion, we must be satisfied with the spontaneous tools we have to forge our union: our recalcitrant secret, tempered with sly lies and subtle cynicism; after all, the balance Father has always talked about applies to everything, wisdom has never been exceedingly virtuous; and not only that, Ana, but in trying to do their best, when has anyone ever reached the core? We can't forget that roads, like all routes, are only cleared on the surface, and that every trace, even life underground, is still only movement over the vast face of the earth; reason is generous, dear sister, it cuts through in any direction, will agree to any byway, as long as we handle the blade skillfully; to live our passion, let us clear our eyes of all artifice, of magnifiers, and of other tempestuous-colored lenses, relying only on their own lucid, transparent water: thus, in our unique love, there can be found no sign of egoism, debasement of custom, nor threat to the species: let us not even worry about such trifles, dear Ana, everything is so fragile, with one superfluous nudge we could push the impertinent curator of the collective virtue aside: and what sort of guardian of the order is he? Standing there haughtily, he's easily caught winking maliciously, and it's impossible to tell whether he's calling our attention to the brazen club in his right hand, or to his lascivious left hand, deep inside his trouser pocket; so let's ignore this pious fraud's pompous edict, it would be feeble of us to allow ourselves to be lulled by such anachronous hypocrisy, after all, is there any bed cleaner than our own nest of hay?" And I braced my muscles forthwith to clear my path, my rodlike arms and iron fists gripping my sabre, which struck away at the inhospitable brush, and as the tips of my spurs scraped the ground, I dispensed with the old tape measure, but, driving in stakes, I sharpened my nerves as if I were sharpening a pencil, doing the arithmetic based on my own figures, little did I care that the grounds from my mind might eventually have had to weigh up against those from another mill: "It's common knowledge, dear Ana, which we ignore like sleepwalkers, but which is, silently, the greatest and oldest scandal of all times: life itself is only organized through contradiction, what is good for some often means death for others, and only the fools among those that have been cast aside would ever borrow the yardstick used by those on top to measure the world; as victims of the order, I insist we have no choice if we want to escape this flaming conflict: we must forge our masks peacefully, draw a scornful mark into the ruby smear of the mouth, and in answer to the choice between forward and backward, we'll even resort to debauchery and run a greased finger along the crack in the universe; if flowers thrive in marshes, we too can dispense with the acquiescence of those unable to grasp destiny's baroque geometry; we can't afford to exchange a precarious situation for no situation at all in the name of discipline, as do the most self-demanding spirits; for my part, I'd even relinquish the possibility of having children, but I want to relish the pleasure of our clandestine love in the old house that much more—" I said, ready to scale steep mountains, after all, I knew how to choose the right harness, curry horses, lead them to a trot, a slow pace and a canter, I mounted well, was agile with the lasso, and could gallop if I had to, not to mention that I also knew how to break in new colts, determining their elegance at the outset, the firm line of their tendons, their steel hooves and their blazing manes—"as a last resort, dear Ana, I appeal to simplicity, answer me reflexively, not from reflection, I entreat you to acknowledge along with me the atavistic line running through this passion: if Father, with his austere manner, wished to make of our home a temple, Mother, with her lavish affection, only managed to render it the house of our damnation," I said, lifting my Sagittarius paws, my hooves kicking up at the beams, suddenly feeling my blood swift

and virulent, immediately whetted over this irreverent voluptuousness; there was grease in my eyes, they were coated
in a dark paste of black smut blended with thick olive oil,
my imagination sent forth a torrent of the most lecherous
images, and my hands, overcome with fever, tore away at
the violent buttons of my shirt, all the way down to my zip;
loftily rediscovering their primitive vocation, they had already become the distant hands of an assassin, confidently
reinstating the rules of a filthy game, liberating themselves
for sweet crime (such orgies!), sweeping across the oratory
in search of flesh and blood, dipping the anemic host into
my wine chalice, scratching into the softness of the lilies in
their vases, leaving my fingerprints on their chaste parch-
ment leaves, combing the alcoves for lascivious saints (such
a coy, crimson-faced virgin! Such pecking at my liver!), and
losing myself in a fog of incense lit in honor of the devil
before me, I said, by then covered with burns, "I'm thirsty,
Ana, I want to drink—" I was but a slab of raw meat— "this
wound, this cancerous fester is not my fault, nor is this
thorn, I can't be blamed for this tumor, this swelling, this
purulence, I'm not to be blamed for these turgid bones, nor
for the mucus flowing from my pores, nor this cursed, hidden slime, I'm not to be blamed for this florid sun, this
crazed flame, I cannot be blamed for this delirium: one
bead on your rosary for my passion, two beads for my testicles, all the beads on this string for my eyes, say ten

rosaries passionately for the brother gone mad!" I foamed fervently, my hands running up and down my exasperated skin, violating my adolescent body and, with whimsical, artful flair, causing my superb, resolute phallus to emerge from the warm, tender flowering of my pubic hair, and filling my hands with the rough scrotum balls hanging below in my groin, the protectors of my primordial fountain of torment, I made a religious offering to my sister of their dense nutrition, but Ana remained impassive, her eyes definitively lost in sainthood, she was a cold, plaster image under that candlelight, and having set myself up for this turbulence from the outset, for a second I fell into dull, ashen anger: "I'm bathed in spleen, Ana, but I can still face your rejection, my violent storm is already perpetually laden with rage, my resistance is strong, plus I've got an alchemist's talent and wisdom, I know how to transform sulfur using the virtue of snakes, and am able to mix dawn's chilly mist into the vapors hovering over the boiling cauldron; I'm planning to cultivate my eyes, everything I see will be planted with barren seed, yielding infertile earth, dirt that will even decay, just as the frost will sear the leaves on the trees, the petals on the flowers and the pulp of our fruit; I won't hide my smile if disease plagues our herds, or our crops, I'll cross my arms while everyone rushes around, turn my back on those asking for my help, cover my eyes so as to avoid their wounds, turn a deaf ear to their cries, and if one day the house tumbles to the ground, I'll shrug my

shoulders; I did not get what I wanted, and I'll have no pity
on the world, to love and be loved was all I ever asked, but
I was cast off without appraisal, amputated, I'm now part of
the dregs, I'm going to surrender, body and soul, to the
sweet delirium of a man who considers himself quite simply
finished at the very onset of manhood, nevertheless, a man
with yet enough strength to dig a deep hole into the rotten
meat of the carcass with his index finger, and to elegantly
close the tropical latitudes and the other lines with his
thumb and ring finger, hurling the skeleton of this world
into a bone pile; now, more than ever, I am a member of the
novel brotherhood of the rejected, the forbidden, the cast-
offs of love, the restless, the quivering, the squirming, the
writhing, the maimed descendants of Cain with their mur-
derous faces (Can't you hear the cavernous ancestry in my
wails?), those with a mark on their forehead, the ancient
ash-scar of sacred envy born by those thirsty for equality
and justice, those who, sooner or later, end up kneeling before the obscure altar of the Malign, after having laid down
their meager offerings before him: a slab of white, cold fish,
black grapes off a rotten vine, the solitary digits of the math-
ematicians, the mute strings of a lute, a handful of desperation and a piece of sacred coal for his creative fingers, offerings for the scrawling craftsman, the aged, scribbling
draftsman, the artisan working from life's castaways, drawing, with his morsel of coal, the extenuated will of each and
every one, and he, the instigator of change, driving us

against the current with his murmurs, scraping our ears'
membranes with his harsh, hot breath, seducing us into
rejecting the precarious solidness of the order, this stone
building whose iron structure, regardless of the architec-
ture, is forever erected on the festered shoulders of the
weeping, he, the first, the only sovereign—your generous
(would that he be discriminating, lousy and revengeful)
God is no more than a vassal, a subaltern, a maker of inad-
equate rules, incapable of perceiving that his very laws are
the resinous wood that fuels the Eternal Fire! The torrent
of my spit is not enough, you must contain this fire while
there's still time, I already feel a new wave coming on, a new
flame licks at me, I sense the onset of desire to torture your
saints, to pierce your tender angels, to bite into the heart of
Christ!" By then, I had taken off, rushing into holy fury,
boils began to cover my body from front to back, I was
drooling vile nettle sap, bleeding the succulent juices of my
cactus, sharpening my teeth to suck the pink liqueur of
boys, desecrating the family shrine at the top of my lungs
(such turbulence running through my mind, such confusion, so much broken glass and how entangled was my
tongue!), but I was abruptly interrupted, Ana stood up in a
violent impulse, the vibration in the air stirring the indecisive candle flames, causing the blazing upheaval in the chapel to falter: I could see the horror in her face, her restrained
fright gradually giving way, and almost at the same mo-

ment, I sensed in her eyes the loving, concerned sister, suffering for me, crying for me, and when I had just barely fallen into the ritual of this old warmth, forever embossed in gold on the spines of sacred books, I suddenly took on the hushed sorrow of the universe, forever embossed in black in the eyes of the sacrificed lamb, I saw myself all at once lying down in a huge grave, surrounded by silent lilies, already asleep in a landscape lined with rows of cypress trees, the density of the uninhabited fields maintained with purple geometry, "I'm dying, Ana," I said, abandoned in hoarse lethargy, covered in the cold fog seeping from the ceiling, hearing the lamenting beefwoods swaying in the wind, and hearing at the same time, a chorus of bizarre voices, the slow moaning of a horn, the rhythmic hammering on an anvil, the dragging of irons and muffled laughter, "I'm dying," I repeated, but Ana was no longer in the chapel.

21

LYING SLUMPED OVER helplessly at the chapel door, my face stuck to the dirt and my neck exposed beneath the darkened sky, for the first time I felt entirely alone in this world; oh! Pedro, my dear brother, it matters not which ancient building, way up on the top, at heights reached only by rare, soaring insects drawing crosses as they swarm the tower (the probing eye of a patient owl emerges from the cavernous night, awaiting me); inside this building erected on atmospheric columns drizzling with bizarre resins, the highest windows always maintain a suspended, mournful gesture; and from the uppermost window, opening out toward rarefied fogs and transparent specters, I install my filaments and antennae, my radar and my pain, and capture space and time in all their calmness, tranquillity and wholeness; I never once doubted there existed, with the same rolling curvature, the same precarious structure, falling with the same weightlessness, a translucent blue breeze, the final bubble of air, found on each new morning leaf, each feather before flight, dense and dripping like dew; but instead of climbing those tower steps, I could simply abandon our home, leave the lands of our *fazenda* behind; the walls and gates of the town were also part of divine right, of all hallowed things.

Homecoming

*"Forbidden to you are your mothers, your daughters,
and your sisters" (Koran, Chapter IV, 23)*

22

". . . AND THE THICKER they make the shell, the more they torture themselves with the weight of the shield, they believe they are safe, but are consumed with fear, they hide from everyone else, all the while unaware that their own eyes wither; they become prisoners of themselves, and never even suspect it, they hold the key, but forget that it opens, and they agonize obsessively over their personal problems, without ever finding a cure, since they refuse the medicine; wisdom is found precisely in not allowing yourself to be closed off in this smaller world: man should be humble, abandon his individuality to become part of a greater whole, whence he draws his grandeur; it is only through the family that each one in this house can enhance his existence, only by giving himself over to the family that each one can find relief from his own problems, and in preserving this union, each one in the family will reap the most sublime rewards; our law is not to withdraw, but to join, not to separate, but to unite, wherever you find yourself, let there also be a brother ..." (From the sermon table.)

23

PEDRO HAD FULFILLED his mission of bringing me back into the bosom of the family; it was a long journey, marked by a difficult retreat, each of us locked inside our own silence throughout the entire trip we took together, during which, like a child, I allowed him to lead me the whole way; it was already nightfall when we arrived, the *fazenda* was sleeping in reclusive stillness, the house was in mourning, all the lights were out, except for a pale clearing on the back patio from the light shining out of the kitchen, where the family was still gathered around the table; we went inside, crossing the front veranda, and as soon as my brother opened the door, the clank of a fork on a plate followed by intense, yet muffled, murmuring preceded the nervewracking sense of expectancy that befell the entire house; I took my leave of Pedro right there in the living room, and went into my old bedroom, while he, his footsteps shaking the china cupboard, disappeared down the hallway to the kitchen, where the family was waiting for him; as I sat on the edge of my old bed, my bags dropped at my feet, I was absorbed by nostalgic aromas awakening vile, mangled images and immersing me in confused thoughts; amidst the ideas running through my mind, I considered the effort Pedro would have been making to hide his pain from everyone, pain perhaps obscured by his fatigue from the journey; upon announcing my return, he couldn't reveal he was bringing home a madman; he would have to put up a tremendous front so that he wouldn't spoil the happiness and joy in my father's eyes, my father, who would soon announce to everyone around him, "He who was lost has returned home, he for whom we have wept has been returned to us."

Frightened by the feverish mood suddenly taking over the back of the house, which was rapidly diffused through the nerves of the walls, along with a mixture of voices, laughter and sobbing, I stood up, dazed, to shut the bedroom door just when it seemed the stern words of the head of the household had checked the emotional outburst; and I could still hear a reverberating, echoing silence when my door was opened, my bedroom light switched on and my father's image appeared in all its rustic majesty, walking gravely toward me; I stood up right away, staring at the floor and suffering the heaviness of his presence before me; I soon felt his gentle hands on my head, running through my hair down the back of my neck and dropping slowly over my shoulders, then he held me to his chest with his strong arms and took my face between his hands to kiss my forehead; once again I was staring at the floor when he said, damp and solemn, "Blessed be this day of your return! Our home has been withering away, my son, but it is once again filled with joy."

And looking at me, holding back his tenderness, studying my tattered features at length, forewarning me of the conversation we were to have a little later on, after everything had calmed down, and also reminding me that I should be restrained with my mother, sparing her, above all, the memory of the days of my absence, my father then told me to bathe, to cleanse myself of the dust from the journey before sitting down to the meal my mother had prepared for me. He had barely let go of me when my sisters burst noisily through the door, throwing themselves at me, hanging from my neck, ruffling up my hair, kissing my face over and over again, running their hands over my back and chest through my shirt, laughing and crying at the same time, all the while rambling on, even awkwardly at times, abruptly revealing that Ana, so pious since my departure, had run to the chapel to give thanks upon hearing the news of my arrival, and that the house had been lit up for the same reason, any passersby would delight in its brightness, and that preparations for tomorrow's fete to celebrate my resurgence were already underway, everyone was to be invited that very night, our neighbors, along with friends and relatives from the village, and that it was the greatest blessing the family had ever received, my homecoming had brought back the lost joy twofold, and filled with warmth and enthusiasm, they pulled me from the room, grabbing me by my arms, and I, gloomy, barely able to conceal my disgusting eyes, let them lead me from the bedroom as they carried on, tenderly flooding me with their silly thoughts, and as soon as we got into the hall, they pushed me through the bathroom door, and sat me down on a crate, and as Rosa, standing behind me, bent over with her arms around my shoulders and started unbuttoning my shirt, Zuleika and Huda, kneeling at my feet, took care of removing my shoes and socks, and as I sat there, surrendering to my sisters' care, I became gradually aware of the zeal surrounding me, the scalding water in the tub had already cooled, there was a cup within reach, a bath towel hanging up, a bar of fragrant soap, rare in our house, a worn-out pair of slippers, not to mention the pajamas, clean and pressed, that I had forgotten under my pillow when I left; I was barefoot and they had already taken off my shirt when they left the bathroom fleetingly, and as Rosa, the eldest sister, closed the door behind her, she warned me I had only five minutes to reappear before the family's eyes, and in the meantime, they were going to make sure our mother was ready to see me.

Disturbed by the turbulence of those caresses, although somewhat revived by the water, I left the bathroom a few minutes later, sensing the softness of my cotton pajamas, my feet comfortable in the loose slippers and the subtle fragrance of the soap on my body. Rosa was waiting by herself, sitting pensively in the living room, she seemed not to notice me when I first walked into the hall, but as soon as she saw me, she came right over, congratulating me on my bath, pulling me toward the living room, her face softened by a calm smile, she, who was so sensible, said, "Listen to me, Andrula: you have to be careful with Mother, she hasn't been the same at all since you left; be generous, brother, don't be sullen with her, at least talk to her a little, but not about anything sad, that's all I ask of you; and now go in to see her, she's in the kitchen waiting for you, hurry up; meanwhile, I'm going to help get ready for your party tomorrow, Zuleika and Huda have already got started, they're beside themselves with joy! God has answered our prayers!" she said, and I felt the sweet pressure of her hand on my back, encouraging me to head down the hallway toward the kitchen, and I was already halfway there when it occurred to me that, although the entire house was lit up, even the bedrooms, it was completely silent and empty, most certainly the family was following Pedro's recommendation, whose persuasive words, given an audience, bordered my father's in terms of authority: I was infirm, required special care and should be spared for the first few hours, not to mention that they had the excuse of my party preparations.

I stopped at the kitchen door: solicitous of all change, rigorously marking the silence, our familiar wall clock was judiciously working through each second; and there was the old, solid, heavy table where the family gathered to eat their daily meals; at the far end, a single place had been set with a white cloth, and on it, the meal that awaited me; my mother was standing next to the head of the table, her broad body motionless, dabbing her eyes with a handkerchief, which she lowered as she sensed my presence; and it was only then I was able to see, despite the light shining through her eyes, how much damage I had done to that face.

24

THIS IS HOW we used to sit around the table for meals, or for sermons: Father at the head, to his right, by order of age, first, Pedro, followed by Rosa, Zuleika and Huda; and to his left, Mother, followed by me, Ana, and then Lula, the youngest. The right branch was a spontaneous growth off the trunk, starting from its roots; the left, though, bore the stigma of a scar, as if Mother, from where the left side started, were an anomaly, a morbid protuberance, a graft on the trunk, perhaps even fatal, it was so weighed down with affection; it might even be said that the places at the table—the whims of time—defined the two lines of the family.

Grandfather, when he was alive, occupied the other place at the head; even after his death, which almost coincided with our move from the old house to the new, it would be an exaggeration to say his chair remained empty.

25

"IT PAINS MY heart to see your face so blemished, son; this is your due for having abandoned our home for a prodigal life."

"Our home is also prodigal."

"What, my son?"

"Our table has always been lavish."

"Our table is laid with moderation and austerity; there's never been any excess, except for holidays."

"But we've always had good appetites."

"We're allowed an appetite without affecting our dignity, as long as it's moderate."

"But we eat until we've no more appetite; that's how we've always left the table."

"Nature is generous in order to satisfy us, placing fruit within our reach, as long as we work to deserve it. If it weren't for our appetite, we wouldn't have the strength to obtain food to survive. Our appetite is sacred, son."

"I didn't say otherwise, it's just that a lot of people work hard, grunting and groaning their entire lives, they wear themselves out, do everything possible, but still can't satisfy their hunger."

"You're speaking strangely, son. No one should despair, often it's only a question of patience, there's no such thing as waiting without reward, how many times have I told you the story of the starving man?"

"I know a story as well, Father, it's also a story about a starving man, a man who toiled from sunup to sundown without ever placating his hunger, and after writhing for so long, his body finally doubled over until he could bite his own feet; surviving at the cost of so many sores, he could but hate the world."

"You've always had a roof over your head here, a bed made up, as well as clean, ironed clothes, food on the table and plenty of affection. You've lacked for nothing. This is why you should forget about these stories of starving men, none of them are relevant now, which makes everything you say seem very strange. Make an effort, my son, try to make yourself clear, don't feign, don't hide anything from your father, it pains my heart to see you lost in so much confusion. For people to understand each other, it's important to have their ideas in order. Word by word, son."

"Inside all order there's a seed of disorder, inside clarity, a seed of obscurity, that's the only reason I talk the way I do. I could be very clear and say, for example, that never, until I decided otherwise, had I ever thought of leaving our home; I could be clear and say furthermore that never, not before nor after I left, did I ever think I would find outside of our home what wasn't given to me inside."

"And what wasn't given to you here?"

"I wanted my place at the family table."

"So, that's why you abandoned us: because we didn't give you your place at the family table?"

"I never abandoned you, Father; all I did, in leaving home, was to spare you the revulsion of watching me survive by eating away at my own insides."

"Yet there was always bread on the table, fulfilling equally the needs of each and every mouth, and you were never forbidden to sit down with the family, on the contrary, that's what we all wanted, that you would never be absent when we broke bread."

"I'm not talking about that, in some cases to participate only in the breaking of bread can be simply cruel: it would merely serve to prolong my hunger; were I to sit at the table for this reason only, I'd prefer to eat bitter bread that would shorten my life."

"What are you talking about?"

"It doesn't matter."

"It was blasphemy."

"No, Father, it wasn't blasphemy, for the first time in my life, I spoke like a saint."

"You're not well, son, a few days' work at your brothers' side will surely break down your proud words, you'll recover your health, right away."

"For the time being, I'm not interested in the health you speak of, sir, there's always a seed of disease therein, just as there's a strong seed of health inside my illness."

"Confusing our ideas is pointless, forget your whims, son, don't try to prevent your own father from discussing your problems."

"I don't believe in discussing my problems, I don't believe in exchanging ideas anymore, I'm convinced, Father, that one plant can never distinguish another."

"Conversation is very important, son, every word, yes, every word is a seed; among all things human capable of leaving us in awe, the strength of the word comes first; even before the use of the hands, it's the foundation for all action, it thrives, and expands, and is eternal, as long as it is just."

"I realize not everyone agrees, but even if I were to live ten lives, in my opinion, the benefits of dialogue, when reaped, are like overripe fruit."

"It's pure selfishness, the natural result of immaturity, to think only of the fruit when planting, the harvest isn't the greatest reward for those who sow; in planting, we have enough gratification knowing that our lives are meaningful, the glory is found in the mere enjoyment of the long gestation period, which is already something valuable we hand down to future generations, if, indeed, we hand the waiting down to future generations, for there is intense pleasure to be found in faith itself, just as there is warmth in the stillness of a bird brooding over eggs in its nest. And there can be so much life in a seed, so much faith in the hands of the planter; it's a sublime miracle that seeds scattered in past millennia, although they have not germinated, have still not died."

"Father, no one lives on sowing alone."

"Of course not, son, if others are to reap what we've sown today, we now reap what's been sown before us. That's how life goes on, such is the current of life."

"And I'm already disenchanted with it, I now know the capacity of this current; those who sow and don't reap, nonetheless, reap what they haven't planted; and I haven't had my share of that legacy, Father. Why keep pushing the world forward? My hands are already tied, I'm not going to choose to bind my feet as well; that's why I really couldn't care less which way the wind blows, I don't see what difference it makes, it doesn't matter whether things move forward or backward."

"I don't want to believe in the little I understand of what you're saying, son."

"You can't expect a prisoner to serve happily in the jailer's house; by the same token, Father, it would be absurd to demand a loving embrace from someone whose arms we've amputated; the only thing that makes less sense is the wretchedness of the maimed person who, lacking hands, applauds his torturer with his feet; or perhaps to be as patient as the proverbial ox that, in addition to the yoke, begs to have the oxbow tightened. The ugly person who cedes to the handsome only becomes uglier ..."

"Go on."

"The poor man who applauds the rich man only becomes poorer; the small man, smaller for applauding the great; the short man, shorter, for applauding the tall, and so on. Whether or not I'm immature, I will no longer recognize values that crush me, I consider it a sad game of make-believe to live inside other people's skin, nor do I understand how there can be nobility in the mimicry of the destitute; the victim crying out in favor of his oppressor makes himself a prisoner twice over, unless of course it's the cynical enactment of a bold pantomime."

"Everything you're saying is very strange."

"It's a strange world, Father, which only unites by dividing; built up on accidents, there is no self-sustaining order; there's nothing more spurious than merit, and I wasn't the one who planted that seed."

"I don't see how these things are related, and even less,

why you're so worried about them. What are you trying to say with all this?"

"I'm not trying to say anything at all."

"My son, you're terribly disturbed."

"No, Father, I'm not disturbed."

"Who were you talking about?"

"No one in particular; I was only thinking of hopeless cases, where there's no cure, of those who cry out in passion, thirst and solitude, who are moaning with good reason; I was thinking only of them."

"I want to understand you, son, but I don't understand anything anymore."

"I'm mixing things up as I speak, I'm familiar with these digressions, the words are carrying me, but I'm lucid, Father, I know where I contradict myself, where I might be out of line, or even overstepping myself, and if there's chaff in all of this, let me reassure you, Father, there are also plenty of whole grains. Even when I'm confusing, I'm not lost; for my own use, I'm able to distinguish the various threads of what I say."

"But you purloin the meaning from your father."

"I've already said I don't believe in discussing my problems, I'm also convinced it's extremely dangerous to shatter intimacy; to me, the larva is only wise while spun in its nucleus, I don't see where it gets its strength once it breaks through the cocoon; it wriggles, of course, and goes through a metamorphosis, all with great effort, only to expose its fragility to the world."

"Rectify your slovenly point of view: it takes strength to face reality; and furthermore, this is your family, you would have to be insane to consider this environment hostile."

"Strong or weak, it depends: reality isn't the same for everyone, and you cannot ignore the fact, Father, sir, that the unfertilized egg doesn't hatch; time is abundant and generous, but it cannot revive the unborn; for those defeated at the outset, for fruit withered at seed, for the downtrodden who haven't ever stood up, there is but one alternative: to turn their backs on the world, to nurture the hope that everything will be destroyed; in my case, all I know is, any environment is hostile, insofar as the right to live is denied."

"You shock me, son, although I don't understand you, I understand your nonsense: there is no hostility in this house, no one here denies you the right to live, it's absolutely inadmissible that such absurd thoughts cross your mind!"

"That's one point of view."

"Refrain from your customary impudence, don't answer in such a manner as to cause me pain. It is not a point of view! Each of us knows our purpose in this household: your mother and I have always lived for you all; you and your brothers and sisters, for each other, no one in need has ever lacked for support in this family."

"Father, sir, you didn't understand me."

"How could I understand you, son? You're stubborn in your denial, and I don't understand that either. Where could you ever find a more appropriate place to discuss the problems causing you so much distress?"

"Nowhere, and even less likely, here; in spite of everything, our family life has always been precarious, there was never room for trespassing certain limits; Father, you yourself said only just now that every word is a seed: it contains life, energy and may even contain an explosive charge: we run great risks upon speaking."

"Don't interpret my words with suspicion and levity, you know very well that you count on our love in this household!"

"The love we've learned here, Father, I discovered only much, much later, knows not what it's after; this indecision makes it of ambiguous value, at this point, no more than a mere hindrance; contrary to belief, love does not always unite, love also separates; and it would make perfect sense for me to state that love in the family may not be as grand as is commonly thought."

"That's enough of your eccentricity, you've gone far enough, your observations are worthless, and your thoughts are chaotic, stop your arrogance, be simple in your use of words!"

"I don't think I'm being eccentric, although it no longer matters to me if I say this or if I say that; but since you think

I am, what difference would it make if now I were to be as simple as the dove? If I were to lay an olive branch down on this table, you, sir, might only see a nettle stem."

"There's no room for provocation at this table, that's enough of your pride, control the snake beneath your tongue, ignore the devil murmuring in your ear, answer me as a son should, above all, be humble in your manner, be clear as a man should be, for once and for all, stop with this confusion!"

"If I'm confusing, if I avoid making myself clear, Father, it's only because I don't want to create further confusion."

"Be quiet! Our water doesn't flow from this fountain, nor our light, from this darkness, your haughty words aren't going to destroy now what it has taken millennia to build; no one in our household will speak with presumptuous profoundness, mixing up words, tangling up ideas, disintegrating everything into dust, because those who open their eyes too wide will only be blinded; furthermore, let no one in our household suffer from a supposed and pretentious excess of light, for it can be just as blinding as darkness; nor should anyone in our household set a new course for that which cannot be diverted, let no one ever confuse that which cannot be confused, the tree that grows and bears fruit with the tree that is barren, the seed that drops and multiplies with the grain that does not sprout, the simplicity of our daily life with unproductive thoughts; I'm telling you to hold your tongue, I will have no depraved wisdom contaminating the ways of this family! It was not love, after all, but pride, scorn, and selfishness that have brought you back home!"

My father mixed so much bitterness in with his anger! And how foolish of me to have exposed the skeleton of my thoughts to him, to have ground a few shavings of bone onto that strange table, so scanty before the powerful strength of his figure at its head.

I was shrunken, and at one point I felt my mother's presence at the kitchen door, checking on the heated discussion, probably trying to interfere in my favor; even without turning around, I could clearly sense the anxiety on her face, begging my father with her anguished eyes, "That's enough, Iohána! Spare our son!"

"I'm tired, Father, forgive me. I admit I'm confused, I admit I was unable to make myself understood, but now I'm going to speak clearly: I have not returned with my heart bursting with pride, sir, as you believe, I've come home humble and submissive, I have no more illusions, I know all about loneliness now, I know about misery, and I also now know, Father, that I shouldn't have ever taken one step beyond our front door; from now on, I want to be like my brothers, I'm going to give myself over to the discipline necessary for my assigned tasks, I'll be out in the field to till before sunlight falls over them, and I'll stay long after sunset; I'll make of my work my religion, of fatigue my inebriation, I'll help preserve the union of the family, from the bottom of my heart, Father, I want to deserve all your love."

"Your words have touched my heart, dear son, I feel new light on this table, tears of joy in my eyes, erasing the bitterness you caused when you left home, erasing all at once the nightmare we've just experienced. For a minute I thought I'd sown long ago in infertile land, in gravel or in a field of thorns. Tomorrow we'll celebrate the son who was blind and has now recovered his sight! So, go rest, it's been a long journey and your homecoming has been filled with emotion, go rest, dear son."

Then I was immediately further compensated for my apparent change of mind: unexpectedly, my mother, who was by then standing behind my chair, took my head in her hands; I surrendered like a child to those thick fingers pressing my cheeks into her breast, my old resting place; leaning over me, she rubbed her eyes, nose and mouth into my hair, smelling it noisily, and spilling out the tender words she had used to address me in her ancient language since I was a child, "my eyes," "my heart," "my lamb," and relaxing in that cradle, I noticed my father heading out into the back yard gravely, as if her effusive tenderness went against his will; he was carrying the same knife he had when he came in, and was now going out in back to join my sisters, who were standing around the rustic table in the shed, caught up in excited flurry, preparing the meats for my party; looking out toward them, I was asking myself why I had come back and I was still unable clearly to discern the dubious outline of my reasons when I noticed, beyond the patio, just inside the woods, Pedro's shadow: with his head bowed, he was walking slowly through the trees, seemingly solemn and taciturn.

26

MY FATHER ALWAYS used to say that suffering is good for man, that it strengthens the spirit and increases sensitivity; he implied that the worse the pain, the greater the opportunity for suffering to play out its most noble role; he seemed to believe that man's resistance was boundless. For my part, I learned when I was very young that it is difficult to determine exactly where resistance ends, and I also learned very young to see resistance as man's strongest trait; but it was also my belief that in strumming the string of a lute—stretched to the limit—a highly tuned note would resonate (assuming that it would be no more than a melancholy, shrill twang), yet it would be impossible to draw any note at all from the same string were it to be stretched until broken. That, at least, is what I thought until the night of my homecoming, having never before suspected that from a broken string, yet a different note could be drawn (which

only confirmed my father's belief that man, even when broken, has not yet lost his resistance, although there is nothing
to prove that he has become still more sensitive).

27

I HADN'T SEEN Ana yet when I turned in (her taking refuge in the chapel upon learning of my return was easily understood), nor my youngest brother, since I had not dared break my silence to ask after his whereabouts. As I entered the bedroom, although I found it somewhat strange, I was not exactly surprised to see Lula in his bed, lying on his side facing the wall, covered by a white sheet from head to toe. The bedroom slept in peaceful penumbra, the clarity from outside the house was diluted, seemed even more calm, diffused as it was by the slats of the Venetian blinds; I didn't turn on the light since I knew my way around the bedroom without difficulty, besides, I had been wearing my pajamas since my bath, so there wasn't much left for me to do: close the door behind me, set my bags over in the corner, kick off my slippers, and slip into bed: weary of scaling mountains, I wanted only to imagine a great grassy plain, to lose myself in drowsiness, to fall sleepily into my dreams, and nightmares, and to wake up the following day with clear eyes, perhaps, as my grandfather used to say, even able "to distinguish a strand of white thread from a strand of black thread in the early dawn light."

Having taken care of the baggage, I immediately noticed that the box I had brought along was missing; still, I didn't give it much thought, even though its contents were so bizarre, the very items I had exposed to Pedro's abashed eyes during that extremely tense encounter back in the distant boardinghouse room; the hemp string had been tossed on to the floor, making me wonder about the hasty hands that had torn open the box without bothering to untie the string (an unheard-of technique in our household) and carried it away only after its contents had been hurriedly studied; sitting there on the bed, I was wrapping the string around my fingers mechanically to save it, using them as a spool in my father's manner, when it crossed my mind that perhaps the box had been stolen to satisfy Lula's pubescent longings; looking over my shoulder to the other bed, I noticed not only was Lula feigning sleep but, with his insolent movements, he was very definitely letting me know that he was not asleep at all, and was merely showing me his full disregard by lying there facing the wall, ostentatiously turning his back on me; I sat there for a good few minutes sounding out his ingenuous, inexhaustible reserve of theatrics while he occasionally kicked away at his sheet, until finally I got up, and walking around my bed, went and sat on his: by then, the sheet was completely still; instead, all of a sudden, I began to hear someone snoring thunderously; slightly surprised at how distracted all of this was making me feel, I put my hand on his shoulder.

"Lula! Lula!"

He took a while to uncover his head and then looked up at me without turning around, grumbling something angrily as if I had just woken him up, and yet, unable to disguise his pleasure.

"Were you asleep?"

"Of course! Couldn't you tell?"

"It's just that I wanted to have a little chat with you, that's all, that's why I woke you up."

"Chat about what?"

"Lula, I've just come home."

"So what?"

"I thought you'd be happy."

"What for?"

"I don't know, I just thought so."

"Well, you thought wrong."

"If that's how you're going to talk, then we'd better just forget it."

"You shouldn't have even started, good night," and Lula pulled the sheet up over his head again, protecting his pride, but he had quit snoring, and had stopped kicking, most certainly expecting me to make another gesture, he seemed anxious to talk with me, he, who had always watched my every move (something I had not known), and for whom I had been a bad example, according to Pedro.

"What's wrong with you, Lula?" I asked, suddenly feeling kind. "I just wanted to talk with you like a friend."

"What's wrong ... what's wrong ... and you have the nerve to ask," he said, without uncovering his head. "I've been here for over an hour, if you must know. An hour! Now you feed me this line about 'friends.'"

"I didn't know, Lula."

"You didn't know ... didn't know ... where else would I be, if you hadn't seen me yet? I wasn't out in the pasture, with the sheep ..." He tried to mollify his refusal, but wouldn't give in.

"OK, Lula, OK. Good night, then," I said, and had barely stood up when he turned around unexpectedly, jerking his sheet, sitting up and leaning his bare chest against the headboard, and delving passionately into the revelation of his bold secret:

"I'm leaving home, André, tomorrow in the middle of your party, but you're the only one that knows."

"Don't talk so loud, Lula."

"I can't stand this prison anymore, I can't stand Father's sermons, nor the work they make me do, nor Pedro's watching over my every move, I want to take charge of my own life; I wasn't born to live here, our herds make me sick to my stomach, I don't like to work the land, not in the sunshine, and much less in the rain, I can't stand the boring life on this filthy *fazenda* anymore ..."

"I said not to talk so loud."

"As soon as you left, André, I started spending all my time sitting up on the gate, dreaming of the open road, looking out as far as my eyes could see, I couldn't take my mind off adventure ... I want to see lots of different cities, travel all over the world, I want to exchange my nosebag for a backpack, become a wanderer, traveling from place to place like a vagabond; I also want to see all the forbidden places, thieves' dens, where money rules the game and wine is drunk by the gallon, where vice runs rampant and criminals plot their schemes; I'm going to have women, I want to be known in the brothels and in the alleys where tramps sleep, I want to do lots of different things, be generous with my own body, experience things I've never experienced; and when I'm left exhausted in the late hours of the night, I'm going to wander the dark streets, feel the early morning dew on my body, watch the day break while stretched out on a park bench; I want to live all this, André, I'm leaving home to take on the world, I'm leaving never to return, I'm not giving in to any pleading, I'm brave, André, I'm not going to fail like you ..."

A rush of dammed-up water (what a current! how frantic!) gushed forth from that adolescent imagination, anxious to spread its poetry and lyricism; most likely, after he had finished describing the plans for his adventures he was hoping for my approval, and while I was listening to all of those fantasies—blown up to useless proportions—I was thinking about lowering his heavily lashed lids and telling him tenderly, "Go to sleep, little boy," but it wasn't to close his eyes that I reached out, running my hand over his smooth chest: I found warm, soft skin, textured like lilies; my imponderable gesture gradually got out of control in that warm resting place, lapsed into unusual searching, making Lula interrupt his speech abruptly, meanwhile, his colt-like legs made up for the silence, reverting to their remarkable stirring under the sheets; and when I reached up to run the back of my hand over his beardless face, his apple cheeks were already feverish; his eyes were a blend of daring and cunning, in one moment advancing, in the next, withdrawing, like a certain other pair of eyes from the past, without any doubt, they were Ana's primitive eyes!

"What are you doing, André?"

Held prisoner in that ancient temple, its feet still covered in salt (such prophecies of turmoil!), I stretched my hand over that young bird which, only moments before, had been beating its wings against the stained glass.

"What are you doing, André?"

I didn't answer the dubious protest, sensing that the sudden cloud of incense filling the room was becoming more and more confused, forming circles, spirals and whirlwinds, obliterating the echoes of the excited, noisy work going on around the patio table, with which several neighbors had joined in. My party was only to take place the following day, and furthermore, I had decided to forestall using any discernment until dawn, not to mention that at sunrise cold dew would also spill out over Lula's beautiful hair, when he would cover the route leading from the house to the chapel.

28

THE EARTH, THE wheat, the bread, our table and our family (the earth); within this cycle, our father used to say in his sermons, there is love, work and time.

29

TIME, TIME, TIME and its inflammable waters, the indefatigable, wide, flowing river, certain of its own slow, curving path, gathering and filtering from all directions the turbid broth of effluents and crimson blood of other channels to build the mystical purpose of history, forever tolerant of the vanity of these feeble, confused instruments, professing to have a hand in determining its course, yet incapable of competing for the riverbed wherein time must flow, and even less capable of flowing individually against the current, woe unto him, Father used to say, who tries to hold back its movement: for he will be consumed by its waters; woe unto him, the wizard apprentice, who tears open his shirt to confront it: he will succumb to its flames, for all change, before daring to utter the name, must be no more than insinuated; time, time, time and its changes, always aware of the larger scheme, and, forever attentive to the finished product, zealous over the smallest details, in every plot, in every inch, in every grain, and also present, with its seconds, in every letter of this passionate story of mine, transforming the dark night of my homecoming into a bright morning, setting the stage from the early hours for the celebration of my Paschal fete, artfully and playfully decorating the rustic landscape around our house, perfuming our still-damp fields, enriching the colors of our flowers, skillfully tracing the lines of its theorem, attracting flocks of doves beneath an enormous blue netting, and also attracting, from the earliest hours, our neighbors, and our relatives and friends from town with their entire families, among them amusing gossips and mischievous children, making up silly games and calling out appropriate greetings, Zuleika and Huda, with the help of girlfriends, were already merrily serving from jugs of wine, repeatedly filling everyone's glasses, laughingly pouring generous, decanted blood into the bodies, always accepted with effusive appreciation, foretelling the rich joy to ensue, and in the woods behind the house, beneath the tallest trees, which along with the sun made up a gentle, joyous play of shadow and light, after the smell of the roasted meat had been long lost among the many leaves of the fullest branches, and the tablecloth, previously laid over the calm lawn, folded away, I curled up near a distant tree trunk, from where I could follow the

tumultuous movements of the group of boys and girls busily getting things ready for the dance, among whom were
my sisters with their country ways, wearing their light,
bright dresses, full of love's promise suspended within the
purity of a greater love, running gracefully, covering the
woods with their laughter, carrying the baskets of fruit over
to the same place where the cloth had been, the melons and
watermelons split open, with gales of laughter, and the
grapes and oranges picked from the orchards lushly displayed in these baskets, a centerpiece suggesting the theme
of the dance, and this joy was sublime, along with the setting sun, porous beams of divine light were easing their way
through the leaves and branches, occasionally spilling over
into the peaceful shadows and reverberating intensely on
those damp faces, and the men's circle then started to form,
my father, his sleeves rolled up, gathered the youngest together, who joined arms stiffly, their fingers firmly intertwined, making up the solid contour of a circle around the
fruit, as if it were the strong, clear contour of an oxcart
wheel, and soon my elderly uncle, the old immigrant, a pastor in his youth, took his flute from his pocket, a delicate
stem, in his heavy hands and began to blow into it like a
bird, his cheeks inflating like those of a child, and his cheeks
swelled so much, got so puffy and flushed, it seemed all his
wine would flow from his ears, as if from a tap, and with the

sound of the flute, the circle began to move slowly, almost obstinately, first in one direction, and then in the other, gradually trying out its strength in a stiff coming and going to the rhythm of the strong, muffled sound of the virile stomping, until suddenly the flute flew, cutting enchantingly into the woods, traversing the blossoming grasses and sweeping the pastures, and the now vibrant wheel sped up, its movement circumscribing the entire circle, which was no longer an oxcart wheel, but a huge mill wheel, spinning swiftly in one direction, and, at the trill of the flute, in the other, and the elderly, who stood by watching, and the young girls, who awaited their turn, were all clapping, strengthening the new rhythm, and when least expected, Ana (whom everyone thought was still in the chapel) emerged impatiently, in a flurry, her loose hair lightly caught up on one side by a drop of blood (such provocative asymmetry!) and spreading torrential flames, fully displaying herself in exuberant debauchery, a greasy smear on her mouth, a charcoal beauty mark on her chin, a purple velvet choker around her neck, a piece of wilted cloth falling like a flower from her exposed cleavage, bracelets on her arms, rings on her fingers, more hoops around her ankles; that was how Ana, covered with the vulgar trinkets from my box, caught my party like a storm, sweeping the dancing circle with her diseased body, confidently introducing her fiery decadence into the center, shocking the surprised looks still further, dangling cries from each of the mouths, paralysing all gestures for an instant, yet still dominating everyone with the violent impetus of her spirit, and right away I could sense, in spite of the greasy oil beginning to darken my eyes, her precise gypsy steps moving about the circle, dexterously and curvaceously weaving her way through the baskets of fruit and flowers, touching the earth only with the tips of her bare feet, her arms lifted above her head in languishing, serpentine movements to the slowest, most undulating melody of the flute, her graceful hands twisting and turning up in the air; she was overtaken with wild elegance, her melodious fingers snapping, as if they were, as if they had been, the first-ever castanets, and the circle surrounding her picked up speed deliriously, the clapping hands outside grew hot and their rhythm strong, then suddenly and impetuously, magnetizing everyone, she grabbed a white handkerchief from one of the boys' pockets, waving it in her hand above her head, all the while sustaining her serpentine movements; this sister of mine knew what she was about, first hiding her venom well concealed beneath her tongue, then biting into the grapes, which hung in saliva-drenched bunches, as she danced amongst them all, rendering life more turbulent, stirring up pain, drawing out cries of exaltation, and presently, harmonizing in a strange language, the elders began to sing out simple verses, almost like chants, and a young mischievous cousin, caught up in the current, made strident cymbals out of two pan lids and it seemed as if, following the contagious music, the herons and teals had flown in from the lake to join everyone there in the woods, and Ana, increasingly bold and daring, came up with a new movement, stretching out her arm, with calculated grace (such devilish versatility!) she stole a glass from one of the bystanders and, in the same instant, spilled the gentle wine over her own naked shoulders, forcing the flute into sudden, languishing regression, drawing acclaim from the onlookers, the crescendo of a choir of muffled voices, at once sacred and profane, the confused communion of joy, agony and torment, she knew how to shock, that sister of mine, how to moisten her dance, soaking her body, chastising my tongue with the liturgical honey of that sweet rapture, hurling me impetuously into bizarre ecstasy, throbbing me into my past, causing me to see my legs to one side and my arms to the other, with amazing lucidity, all of my appendages amputated and searching out for each other within the ancient unity of my body (I was rebuilding myself in this pursuit! Such brine in my sores, such wholesome burning in this rhapsody!), I was then certain, more certain than ever that it was all for me, that she was dancing only for me (time's great turnaround! Such a bone, such a deadly thorn, such glory for my body!), and sitting on an exposed root over in a shady corner of the woods, I let the light wind blowing through the trees flow through my shirt, inflating my chest, and felt the soft caress of my own hair on my fore-head, and from a distance, in this apparently relaxed posi-tion, I imagined the lavender aroma of her fresh complex-ion, the full tenderness of her mouth, like a piece of sweet orange, and the mystery and malice in her date-like eyes; my staring was unabashed, I untied my shoes, took off my socks and, with my clean, white feet, scraped away the dry leaves to the thick humus below, and my unrestrained de-sire was to dig into the earth with my nails and to lie down in this pit and cover myself with the damp earth, and, lost on this secluded trail, initially I barely perceived what was happening, in my confusion, I first noticed Pedro, still taci-turn up to that point, searching everywhere with a deranged look in his eyes, stumbling blindly among the magnetized bystanders in that marketplace — the flute played on deliriously, frantically, the snake in her belly played on de-liriously, frantically, and standing up, I watched as my brother, more crazed than ever, located my father and fled in his direction, then, yanking his arm, and pulling him to-ward him violently, he shook him by the shoulders as he wailed his somber revelation, sowed that deranged seed into my father's ears, secreting his excruciating pain, his cries and agony (poor brother!), and time, playing out the concert theme exquisitely, finished it off by halting the hands on the clock: corrupt currents set in flawlessly at several points, searing the atmosphere as they flew, leaving our trees barren, parching the green from our fields, staining our bulging stones with rust, prematurely creating space for the many cactus towers soon to be built in majestic solitude: my father's noble forehead, he himself still glistening with wine, glowed for an instant in the warm sunlight as his entire face was bathed in unexpected, horrible white, and from that moment on everything gave way, lightning struck with deathly speed: the cutlass was within his reach, and severing the group with the onslaught of his fury, my father, in one fell swoop, struck the oriental dancing girl (such purposeful red, such a cavernous silence, such a sordid chill in my eyes!), a lamb going up in flames would not have been as momentous, nor the exasperated demise of any other member of the herd, but the patriarch himself, wounded at his very maxims, the patriarch now possessed by divine wrath (poor Father!), the guide himself, the tables, the law itself had gone up in flames—this fibrous, palpable material was so solid, not bare-boned as I had always imagined, it had substance and there was red wine running throughout, it was bloody, resinous and reigned drastically over our pain (ours was a pitiful family, to be prisoner of such solid phantoms!), and from the deadly silence that collapsed behind that gesture, there emerged right away, like a primitive birthing wail

Father!

and from a dif-
ferent voice, a densely desperate, hollow moan, Father!

and from everywhere,
from Rosa, from Zuleika, and from Huda, the same defence-
less weeping

Father!

it was strangulated bleating

Father! Father!

where is our shelter? where is our protection?

Father!

and from Pedro, prostrate on the
dirt

Father!

and then I saw Lula, still a child, and yet so crazed, writhing
on the ground

Father!

Father!

where
is the union of our family?

Father!

and I watched my mother,
losing her grasp on her mind, pulling out her hair by the fist-
ful, grossly baring her thighs, exposing the purple cords of
her varicose veins, beating her stone-like fists against her
breasts

Iohána! Iohána!

Iohána!

and all the cries for help
were to no avail, and, refusing any consolation, wandering
among those crushed, murmuring groups as if she were lost
among ruins, Mother began to wail in her own language,
drawing out an ancient lament that to this day can still be
heard along the poor Mediterranean coast: there was lime,
and there was salt; her cragged plea carried the sand-filled
pain of the desert.

30

(IN MEMORY OF my father, I transcribe his words: "and every once in a while, each one in the family should take time from more urgent tasks to sit down on a bench with one foot planted squarely on the ground and, bending over, your elbow resting on your knee and head resting on the back of your hand, with gentle eyes, you should observe the movement of the sun, the wind, and the rain and, with these same gentle eyes, observe time's mysterious manipulation of the other tools it wields to effect all transformations, and you must never once question its unfathomable, sinuous designs, just as upon observing the pure geometry of the plains, you would never question the winding trails shaped by the trampling of the herds out to pasture: the cows always head for the watering pit.")